Readers love the Alchemists and Elementals series by CASSIE SWEET

Eye of Truth

"If you enjoy the magic of alchemy, epic battles, intrigue and secret orders then you should check this one out."

—Gay List Book Reviews

"This book was fantastic; I loved every minute of it."

—The Romance Reviews

"An absolutely wonderful start to a new fantasy series …"

—Gay List Book Reviews

Taste of Air

"Rest assured it is well-crafted and multi-dimensional to the point where I found it all but impossible to put this book down."

—It's About the Book

"… it is easy to lose yourself in the magical fantasy world Ms. Sweet has invented. It is an amazing world where elemental powers, magic and necromancy are set in a medieval time period."

—Crystal's Many Reviewers

Hot Water

Cassie Sweet

Dreamspinner Press

Published by
DREAMSPINNER PRESS

5032 Capital Circle SW, Suite 2, PMB# 279, Tallahassee, FL 32305-7886 USA
http://www.dreamspinnerpress.com/

This is a work of fiction. Names, characters, places, and incidents either are the product of author imagination or are used fictitiously, and any resemblance to actual persons, living or dead, business establishments, events, or locales is entirely coincidental.

Hot Water
© 2014 Cassie Sweet.

Cover Art
© 2014 Christy Caughie.
Cover content is for illustrative purposes only and any person depicted on the cover is a model.

All rights reserved. This book is licensed to the original purchaser only. Duplication or distribution via any means is illegal and a violation of international copyright law, subject to criminal prosecution and upon conviction, fines, and/or imprisonment. Any eBook format cannot be legally loaned or given to others. No part of this book may be reproduced or transmitted in any form or by any means, electronic or mechanical, including photocopying, recording, or by any information storage and retrieval system, without the written permission of the Publisher, except where permitted by law. To request permission and all other inquiries, contact Dreamspinner Press, 5032 Capital Circle SW, Suite 2, PMB# 279, Tallahassee, FL 32305-7886, USA, or http://www.dreamspinnerpress.com/.

ISBN: 978-1-63216-467-4
Digital ISBN: 978-1-63216-468-1
Library of Congress Control Number: 2014947926
First Edition December 2014

Printed in the United States of America
∞
This paper meets the requirements of
ANSI/NISO Z39.48-1992 (Permanence of Paper).

To all those who found love without ever looking.

Acknowledgments

I'D LIKE to thank Marguerite Labbe for her constant and unfailing encouragement on this venture of mine. Your friendship means so much.

Chapter One

THE BEST thing on a hot summer night was the forbidden taste of a new lover's lips. Clive Ducaine dove in for another sample.

Christ, this guy was thermonuclear.

What was his name? Clive couldn't remember at the moment. His head was too filled with the sharp tang of musk and a subtle hint of sandalwood. The abrasive scrub of stubble against his lips made a moan catch in the back of his throat. He loved that sensation. Craved it.

Music from the pool area at the nearby resort filtered down to the stand of palm trees where Clive had taken his hookup. God, he was so on fire he couldn't even remember the dude's name. The guy was one of those uptight corporate types who came down to Santa Juanita for some sun and relaxation.

All the better. Clive wasn't given to wanting anything to last past the length of the average vacation. A week—two weeks tops.

Hookup snaked his hands up under Clive's shirt and left a wake of heated skin. He moaned into Clive's mouth and stepped forward a little, grinding their erections together.

Oh, hot damn. Clive was about to explode. Good thing the baggy carpenter shorts he wore left room for expansion. He didn't think his cock had ever been so hard and in need of attention.

Clive backed Hookup against a palm tree and continued the kiss. Their tongues danced and mouths slanted, each trying to declare dominance. Clive wasn't about to let the tourist win. This was *his* island. *His* paradise. He'd made it his sworn duty to show the vacationers what temptations the tiny South American resort had to offer. What sensual delights awaited them in the perfumed nights.

He moved his hands over Hookup's steely chest and broke the kiss only long enough to pull the man's shirt over his head. Olive skin with a slight hint of a tan glistened in the light coming from the resort. A faint dusting of dark hair spread out over perfectly sculpted pecs. A single line of hair marched downward to disappear under his waistband. Off to the right, the rigid outline of his erection was visible behind the thick denim of his jeans.

Clive ran a bent knuckle over the flat coins of Hookup's nipples. They hardened into small points. He dipped his head and flicked one a few times as he sent his hand down the front of Hookup's body.

"Holy fuck." Hookup's voice eased between his teeth on a loud breath.

"It will be," Clive assured him. He'd never gotten one complaint in all his years. His lovers walked away satisfied.

Or just walked away. He cut off the bitter thought as if it had never popped into his head.

He pushed the ragged memory away and started to finesse Hookup's button open on the top of his fly. He took Hookup's mouth again as he put his hand down into the front of Hookup's pants.

Hookup moaned and eased his hips forward. "God, that feels good."

It was going to feel even better in a minute. Clive swirled his finger around the head of Hookup's penis.

Suddenly Hookup's entire body stiffened, and he broke away from Clive's mouth. "I can't do this" came out on a ragged breath.

What!

Clive might have screamed that in his head. The guy was right on the verge and running hot. From the way Hookup moved his hips back and forth while Clive massaged him, he was ready for the next act. Stop? That didn't even compute at the moment, and yet he'd heard it loud and clear.

Clive took a step away and held up his hands in the air. Never let it be said that he pushed when a potential lover put on the brakes. He wasn't that kind of guy. Didn't need to be. The resort had any number of men passing through on a daily basis who would love to come back to his bungalow with him and spend the night twisting the sheets into sailor's knots.

That didn't stop Clive's heart from thundering in his neck and ears and his breathing from coming out in labored pants between his teeth. He'd been more than ready to throw down with the guy.

Despite the normally rich selection of potential lovers, this season the prospects had been poor, the tourists either already paired off or horribly straight.

Hookup picked up his shirt from the ground and shook the sand out of it. "I'm sorry."

Clive wasn't going to cry over it, though it chapped his pride pretty damn hard. He shrugged, pretending it didn't matter. "Fine."

He pulled his keys out of his pocket, moved his shirt to hide his erection—not that it mattered much now, as the damn thing was going down with the sting of rejection. Still, if he cut through the resort on his way to the main road, he didn't want his friends and coworkers to see him with the lone boner of the apocalypse.

Shit. Now he'd have to go back to the bungalow and jack off. The last thing he wanted was to go to bed unsatisfied and then lie there all night and stare at the ceiling asking himself why. Rejection, even at thirty-five, still felt like a knee to the balls. Even if he couldn't remember the guy's name.

Clive turned and walked back through the stand of trees that separated the garden from the main pool area. The fiesta was still raging full blast. People crowded the dance floor, bumping and grinding to a Latin dance beat.

He loved it here. Some days more than others. Overall, moving an entire continent away and succumbing to paradise had been a good decision for him.

Across the floor, his friends were all seated at a table, laughing and drinking. On fiesta nights the resort employees were invited to share in the festivities. As a matter of fact, the management greatly encouraged the practice. As a private vendor and contractor, he wasn't really a resort employee as much as an associate, but he did use their marina to run his dive business and as such felt an obligation to attend functions.

Tonight, however, was a different story. He had made his appearance, and now he could leave without feeling as if he'd totally blown the night off. Even if it wasn't going to end the way he'd anticipated.

Win some. Lose some. He'd vowed a long time ago not to beg anyone to stay with him, and he didn't intend to break that over a random hookup at the resort. No matter how hot the guy or how smokin' his body.

Clive scooted out of the pool area and to the front of the resort without his friends being the wiser. With any luck no one would ask about Hookup next time he saw them. If so, he'd give his standard shrug and say nothing.

He might take serious delight in the banquet of buff bodies and tanned skin that usually hung around the marina, but he wasn't one to kiss and tell. It had never been his style, no matter how often his friends begged him for details.

The walk home was over a mile. The road was dark and deserted for this time of night. He stayed to the road, since the waterfront had jetties stringing off the beachhead that made crossing that way at night treacherous. Still, getting hit by some drunk wasn't a fun proposition either, so he stayed as close to the tree line as possible.

It wasn't too late. Most of the locals would be at home, getting ready for bed and the workday in the morning. The tourists were either at Villa la Vita for the fiesta or one of the other many resorts that dotted the coastline.

Only one or two cars passed him on his trek. Good. He didn't want to run into anyone he knew. Locals would often stop and offer him a ride if they saw him on foot. More often than not he rode his bike down this stretch. It was good exercise in low gear. Especially with the way the last hundred yards to his place was up a steep hill overlooking a bluff.

Great exercise, actually, and also good for working off any unspent steam he might have—though, tonight he had another kind of heat to work off.

Shit. What had he done to push the guy away or turn him off? Hadn't he mentioned that Clive's caresses felt good? Maybe the guy had some weird complex about feeling good. If so, he'd come to the wrong damn place for vacation.

He'd seen it time and again. Corporate suits came down here with their pasty skin and high-tech gadgets and acted like those who lived on the island were too unsophisticated to realize they had come seeking salvation from a merciless world. Well, they wouldn't find it here if they didn't look. No one put happiness on a platter at the fiesta buffet and dished it up by the spoonful. People had to dive in and find it for themselves. Clive knew. He'd escaped that kind of office prison hell a long time ago. He preferred his life laid-back, uncomplicated, and spent in perpetual paradise.

When he stepped up on his porch, he noticed the white piece of resort stationary taped to his door. What the hell? Why hadn't someone just flagged him down and given it to him at the fiesta? It would have made more sense.

He tore the paper off and went inside. Light from the brilliant half-moon lit the back of the house, casting a muted glow over the white sheers covering the sliding glass doors. He clicked on a light and opened the piece of paper.

Early morning call. Divers want out by 7. See you then. J.P.

Probably was a good thing he hadn't brought Hookup home with him. Seven came way too early on the island. Most people didn't start to stir until eleven. It wasn't that kind of place. The hustle and bustle of the city was far away. This was a spot for relaxing and enjoying every sensation imaginable. God, he hated it when off-islanders came down and insisted on doing things at the crack of dawn. Rocks weren't even awake at seven. Not to mention, he had no idea if the people he was taking out were experienced divers. It made a big difference.

The last thing he wanted was a bunch of amateurs getting their asses killed because they were too inexperienced to heed warnings or pay attention to their surroundings. Hopefully Juan Pablo had screened the divers before accepting the fee. He'd hate like hell to refund the chunk of money they had to have laid down for securing him as a tour guide that early in the morning.

"You're a stupid fucker." The insult came from the corner of the room and was followed by a whistle.

"Yeah, thanks for that." Clive crossed the room to his blue parrot and ran a finger down the bird's chest. "I appreciate it, especially tonight."

"Stupid fucker. Stupid fucker."

Clive chuckled. He'd found the poor bird hopping along the ground at the resort. Some asshole had broken its wing. It was nearly dead from dehydration and hunger when Clive had come across it. After a trip to a vet and some major TLC, Clive had brought the bird home. At the time he'd not known the bird's love of English profanity.

Rodger cooed softly at the attention.

"You hungry, buddy?"

"Tastes like shit."

He got the bird food out and placed some in the dish. The water still looked clean and fresh, so he'd leave that until morning.

"Seven comes pretty early, Rodg. I'm going to have to grab some sheet soon." He held out his hand, and the bird stepped onto the side of it. "But I have some time to spend with my favorite little dude."

"Ballbuster."

"I'm not the only one."

Clive walked to the sofa and sat down. He transferred the parrot to the back of the sofa, where a removable runner kept the furniture from getting ruined.

He stretched out his legs. When he turned his head to the side, he got a huge whiff of sandalwood and spice cologne. His head spun and dick hardened. Damn the guy had smelled good.

He lifted his shirt and sniffed at the collar. The scent had rubbed off onto the fabric. Instead of sitting there in acute torture, he ripped off the offending garment and threw it as far as it would go.

Like he needed the reminder the evening hadn't turned out with him getting off with a hot stranger. The guy was probably frigid or had a significant other or had come to the island on the down low. Wouldn't be the first time some dude came to Santa Juanita and wanted to experience a walk on the other side that no one back home would know about. Clive tried not to be a party to those types of entanglements. He never wanted to be anyone's experiment or dirty little secret. He had too much self-respect for that bullshit.

He scratched Rodger behind the crown and along the side of his yellow mask. The bird turned its head in little trills of ecstasy.

"Who's the pretty boy?"

"Jolly Rodger." The bird lolled its head in the other direction.

"That's right. He's a good boy."

Clive spent another few moments enjoying the quiet of his little bungalow and the affections of a bird who gave nothing but love in exchange for a few handfuls of sunflower seeds and fresh water. Animals had it right.

He could have killed the fucker who had maimed the beautiful little guy. Rodger turned his head and started plucking at Clive's hair with his beak. The bird did that whenever he was being especially affectionate.

"You want to go out on the boat with me in the morning?"

"Arrrr."

THE GUY had vanished.

One moment he was moving through the trees to the poolside, and the next he'd gotten lost in the crowd.

Trevor Donohue glanced around the pool area. People were jammed on the dance floor. Music flooded out of the speakers, sending the vibration of heavy bass through his feet. Food and drinks flowed freely to the resort's guests, most of whom looked like they were having a great time.

He had been, too, until he'd opened his big mouth and sent the guy running off into the night. That wasn't what he'd meant to do. He'd just wanted to put the brakes on for a bit. Slow down and take a breath. Things were moving too fast, heading into territory he was sure he'd regret come morning.

Hell, he hadn't even been on the island for four hours and he'd scored a major hit with one of the sexiest guys he'd ever seen in his life. His mouth had actually gone dry when he'd first seen Surfer Boy come into the poolside bar, walking with a confident air and smelling like ten kinds of sin.

A kick of desire had scored him low in the belly. He was not the type to indulge in one-night stands or brief affairs. He'd been there and done that too many times to count. No one even came close to what he'd lost. Not that he'd been looking to replace Jason. Not that he ever could. Lately, however, he'd been so busy he didn't have time to date, let alone form any sort of lasting relationship. Lately, he'd lived like a monk, save for the jar of hand cream on his nightstand.

Damn, his hands were still shaking, and his dick was hard as a rock. He'd kept his shirt out of his pants to hide the evidence of his hard-on. Without the benefit of looking into a mirror, he knew his hair stood up in passionate disarray. He ran a hand through it to try and regain some semblance of order.

Where had Surfer Boy gone? The guy moved like the wind. Or maybe the sun had gotten to Trevor and he'd only imagined the tanned god with the secret smile and shoulders to die for.

Great, now he felt like a piece of bad meat—chewed up and thrown away like gristle. Without an explanation, either. Surfer Boy had simply put his hands up and walked away, as if they hadn't just shared a really intense encounter.

And it had been intense—major league intense. In all caps with neon lights and sparklers going off around it. One moment Trevor had been sitting on a lounge chair on the other side of the pool, nursing a beer, and the next he was being chatted up by a guy who'd stepped out of a surfing fantasy.

Trevor should have kept his mouth shut except to suck some tongue.

He rubbed a hand over his heart where it still thumped a little too wildly.

Laughter from a corner table captured his attention. A group of people stared at him as if they knew what he'd been doing. Not that he was ashamed. Hell, he'd been out for years and owed no one an explanation or apology for his life. He was comfortable in his skin and sexuality.

He pulled his shirt down to make sure it covered his fly and left the pool area. The fiesta had lost its luster. Not even the colorful decorations, delicious food, or lively music could tempt him to rejoin the party.

Trevor passed through the lobby and up to the great glass elevator. Up on the mezzanine level of the lobby, a window stretched from one side of the main room to the other, giving guests a panoramic view of the marina. The half-moon sparkled on the water. Stars shimmered in the cloudless sky. It was a night for romance.

His stomach rolled and pitched at his stupidity.

All he had to do was open up to the possibility of romance and it would have been his for the taking. But no, he had to be Mr. Pragmatic and put a stop to it like some damn Victorian maiden. And why? Because he was worried about what kind of an example he'd make for the company? Trevor had always lived his life by certain standards. As the vice president of a medical manufacturing and durable goods company, he wanted to be an example for his employees. He also had a hard time accepting that something good might walk into his personal life.

Damn. Halfway around the world and he still couldn't shake the specter of that one damn night when life had turned him up by the heel and shaken him hard. It had a way of creeping up on him at the oddest times, sucking the joy out of life.

Did he even deserve to feel good and enjoy his vacation?

That was why he'd pushed Surfer Boy away—a deep fear of losing control. Of appreciating pure bliss and living in the moment, of doing something for himself alone without regard for anyone else. Down in his heart of hearts he knew he didn't deserve to be happy.

Hard work and long hours were his penance for having survived that horrible night eight years ago.

The elevator dinged and the doors opened. He took his keycard from his pocket and started down the long hallway.

Laughter rose from the lobby level. At least some people were having a good time. What was the use of coming to paradise alone? None.

God, he felt old for thirty-five.

Old and tired.

He let himself into the room and glanced around.

It was a nice suite. No one could argue otherwise. There was a big living room decorated in airy colors, and a bathroom with marble counters and gold fixtures. He kept going to the back of the suite and into the bedroom. He walked over and opened a set of double doors that led to a balcony. Wind off the water rippled the sheers and sent them dancing.

The bedroom had a second bathroom, just as grand as the first one. But where the first had a shower and tub, this one only featured the shower stall.

He crossed the room and clicked on his computer. So what if he'd promised Geoff he wouldn't even open e-mail while he was away. How was he supposed to survive an entire month without reading his e-mail? What if something urgent came in? How was he supposed to keep in touch with the outside world if he didn't have e-mail access? And then there was that deal with the Danish company and the red tape holdup with the FDA regulators. The entire deal was becoming a fucking nightmare. Trevor had cautioned that the company might be better served to develop their own similar product, but he'd been told it was too expensive.

Trevor ran a hand through his hair. It had been a really bad time for Geoff to force Trevor into a vacation. A horrible one. However, if the deal went sour, Trevor could always point the finger and say "I told you so."

He typed in his account and was disappointed to see no new e-mails since he'd last checked. What the hell? Had the employees forgotten he was the VP? That his continued good opinion of them mattered to their careers at Global? Geoff had probably told them all not to contact Trevor for any reason.

Trevor gazed out of the balcony window at the spectacular night. Oh, yes. Give him boardrooms and meetings with a full list of projects and clients to handle and he was in heaven. Send him on a weeklong conference to some godforsaken part of the States where the food was bad and accommodations lousy and he was all right with it, but for crying out loud, don't send him to an island with nothing to do and no contact with the company. It was his own personal version of hell.

Geoff might have said he had Trevor's health and well-being in mind, but Trevor doubted it. This was more like torture. Torquemada should have used this at the Inquisition.

Having nothing to do always brought with it scenes out of time and place. Doubts stirred in his head and heart and put him right back on that darkened street in the Village, the pop of gunfire, and Jason falling into Trevor's arms covered in blood. The frantic rush to help stanch the blood and the futile attempt at CPR. None of it had mattered in the end. Not one thing had changed the outcome.

He sat on the bed and removed his shoes and socks, then stripped down to his underwear. Sorrow lodged in his heart, making a damn big lump that he swore one day would make his heart stop beating altogether. Or maybe he only wished it would.

He lay back against the pillows and turned out the light.

The sea breeze coming off the water was cool enough to keep the room comfortable. Not long after he lay down, he fell into a deep, troubled sleep.

Chapter Two

HOT SUN bore down on Clive's shoulders as he packed his gear away in his duffle. The tanks were already stored on the boat and the regulators in their proper places. As divemaster he was extremely particular about the gear and always made sure it was cleaned and secured before taking care of the other less important articles he used on a dive.

Spray from the deep blue waters of the Atlantic blew into his face as the dive boat sped toward the marina. He looked up as the resort came into view. It appeared as a series of white dots against the hillside. Not much to look at from the distance, but to him it was perfection.

The woman in the orange bikini kept giving him the eye. Even with her sunglasses on, he felt the weight of her stare on his midsection. If he'd been a lesser man, he'd have told her that no amount of seductive poses or soft coos was going to turn his head. Now, the man she was with was a different story.

The guy was chiseled and taut for a silver fox, with a deep tan and just the right amount of crow's feet to make him interesting. He was also blatantly heterosexual. Clive didn't have to be a mind reader to know that, he only had to watch the way the man tracked every pretty, swimsuit-clad woman who walked by.

Living on a resort island brought all manner of people into his life. He tried not to get tangled up with most of them. It was a sixth sense he had that made him able to ferret out the ones who just wanted a quick roll from those who came to the island looking for love.

He wished the brochures on the mainland and all the way in North America would stop making the place look like *Fantasy Island*. He'd lived on Santa Juanita for years, and he'd never met one person who resembled Mr. Roarke. People came down to the island for different reasons, but they all left feeling a little closer to heaven.

"Do you ever go to the resort bar at night? Is there a lot of action?" Orange Bikini sidled up to him and leaned against the railing. This close he could tell she'd had some work done around her mouth. It was pulled just a little too tight to be natural. He had to commend her, though—for an older lady, she had a very nice figure.

He glanced over her shoulder to her partner, who was busy chatting up a brunette in a red thong.

"Very rarely."

"Make this one of the exceptions."

Clive nodded in the direction of the silver fox. "Is he your husband?"

She turned and looked in her partner's direction. "Boyfriend, but we have a very open relationship."

"How open?"

She smiled and ran the tip of her tongue over her lips. "We've agreed to hook up where we can on this vacation. No questions asked."

"Will *he* be at the bar?"

She frowned and pursed her lips. "Oh. I see."

He gave her a charming but crooked smile. "Like Popeye, I am what I am."

She gave a heavy sigh, which raised her medically enhanced boobs higher than what should have been physically comfortable. Her cheeks were red, and he doubted they were sunburned, since she was already tanned as a piece of wheat toast. "You're just too hot to be gay."

"I didn't realize there was a cutoff on looks." Clive laughed and put a companionable arm around her. "Cheer up. There will be plenty of hot guys at the bar who are going to stand in line to take you up on your offer."

"Oh yeah? Do you know any?"

Call it the last of his romantic streak, but he gave a head bob to the silver fox. "Why not hook up with your boyfriend? You came all the way down here with him for a reason. Might as well make it count."

She looked away from her boyfriend and thong-girl. "He's about to trade me in for a newer model."

"He might think you're about to do the same."

Juan Pablo slowed the boat and pulled up to the dock. Clive jumped out to help secure the line and ensure the passengers disembarked safely.

Rodger sat on his shoulder bobbing his head and offering a very tame, *"Thank you. Come again,"* as the tourists departed. The feisty bird waited until they were out of earshot to say *"Assholes."*

Clive *tsked*. "You shouldn't say that, buddy. Their money helps keep you in birdseed."

"Living on peanuts."

He scratched the bird and laughed. "Come on. Let's go home."

"Home. Home."

He grabbed his gear, said good-bye to the crew, and climbed up the hill to the bike rack near the parking area.

The duffle converted to a backpack that he slipped his arms through and secured on his back. Rodger climbed into the little basket upfront, where he rode shotgun. A picture of the pirate flag Jolly Rodger was painted on the basket. Instead of the classic human skull with the eye patch, Clive had painted a parrot skull. Rodger seemed to like the artwork and rode in his basket with pride.

The sky was clear and pristine on the ride home. His mind churned with the conversation he'd had with the tourist. He hated explaining himself. He also hated giving false hopes to people. In the end it got embarrassing for both parties. It was best to just cut to the chase and let them know up front that he wasn't interested.

Clive had been interested last night, but that hadn't worked out so well. Had he been too aggressive? Hookup was just too luscious for words and obviously not into quick rolls without strings.

One-night stands, flings, short affairs that were over in a week were more Clive's style. Anything longer led down a rocky road of disaster and heartache. The only lovers he met these days were transient in his life, and he liked it that way. Strict personal policies kept him from dating people with whom he worked. That usually got sticky and uncomfortable if things went bad. Really, there were no other alternatives besides tourists or the occasional businessman on the mainland in Brazil.

As he pedaled down the lane to his home, the thought of hanging out in the bar sounded good. He could use some company, especially tonight. Not that he didn't appreciate Rodger's offhanded and profanity-laden conversations, but he'd rather spend some time with beings who spoke with more than four-letter words.

Getting rejected and thrown away like a cheap opportunist had left a bad mark on his otherwise pristine fling matrix. Clive needed to find someone to help ease the burn. Maybe then he'd get back on track with his love 'em and see 'em later attitude.

He needed to come up with a plan of some kind to turn Hookup's head. Make him see what he'd missed the night before.

Wait a minute? What was he thinking?

Clive hadn't used that MO when he'd been kicked to the curb ten years ago. He sure as hell wasn't going to start doing it now.

Maybe he'd simply be nice and see if that brought Hookup back. If the dude wanted to take it slow, Clive had all the time in the world. It wasn't like he was going anywhere.

ANOTHER POOL party. It was the most interesting thing the day had to offer. Renewed and rested after a nice long nap, despite the nightmares of going home to find Geoff had promoted Thompson to VP, Trevor went downstairs to the pool bar. There was an open buffet with plenty of food and two-for-one margaritas.

He passed on the drink special and went straight for a Scotch on the rocks. The bar was hopping for a weeknight, but then, all these people were on vacation, and there wasn't such a thing as the weeknight work schedule.

People swarmed the dance floor, and others played in the pool. A Latin club mix pounded out a sensual beat as bodies writhed in time to the music. He felt the bass all the way into his groin and deeper. The air seemed to be alive.

Conversations in Spanish and Portuguese peppered the air around him. He'd wondered, with Santa Juanita being so close to Brazil, why the island's first language was Spanish. It didn't make sense until he'd read a bit about the history in the resort packet in his room. The island had originally been settled by the Spanish, who had controlled Santa Juanita until the islanders claimed independence back in the early 1900s. Cultural influences of many different nations were represented in the sights, sounds, and smells of the resort. People from all over the world came here to relax and unwind from the cares of their daily lives. All but Trevor. He stuck out like a nightmare in a happy factory.

A man stepped into the pool area looking like the God of Sun and Surf. His blond Adonis good looks were worthy of a pinup poster, and his tan proclaimed him an avid beachgoer. Oh God, it was Surfer Boy.

Panic seized Trevor for a half breath. What the hell was he going to say? How was he going to earn back his man cred?

Heat speared him from head to balls. Trevor watched from the corner of his eye as Surfer Boy approached the bar. Surfer Boy nodded to the bartender, who opened a cooler and retrieved a beer without a word ever being exchanged. The guy must be a regular.

Trevor assessed the man as the memory of hot flesh tingled his fingertips. The body under the soft white cotton shirt was muscular and fit. His baggy khaki shorts failed to hide his well-shaped thighs and trim waist. All right, so the guy was perfection. So what? It didn't mean if he opened his mouth anything of importance or sense would come out.

Though he'd sounded pretty sensible the night before. As a matter of fact, he'd shown a good dose of humor, sarcasm, and fun. It was a lethal combination for Trevor. He'd always gone for the ones who could make him laugh. Maybe that's why none of the guys he'd dated since Jason had worked out—they simply didn't make him feel that good. Not as good as Surfer Boy.

He shot another surreptitious look at the beach god. Oh yeah. He was hotness personified.

Trevor took a sip of his drink to wet his suddenly dry throat.

Damn, he just couldn't stop staring at the man. Surfer Boy was that luscious. That confident. That melt-you-into-a-puddle-of-rutting-sex hot.

Surfer Boy nodded and tipped his beer at Trevor in salute. Trevor gave a nod and felt his insides go tight as the man eased his way down the bar and lounged casually against the rail. He turned to watch the people at play in the sultry heat. Surfer Boy's thigh was a ghost of a brush against Trevor's.

This was not going to go well. Trevor was not about to be forced into an apology, or to speak first.

"Let me guess," Surfer Boy said in a husky voice that shot heat straight to Trevor's balls. "You like to take it nice and slow?"

Amazed that Surfer Boy was so perceptive, Trevor gave a pained smile. "How can you tell?"

"You corporate types are all alike. Pale, drawn, and look like you could use a few wild nights and a good tan. But when push comes to shove, you're all just talk."

"I've never been accused of being pale," Trevor huffed. "At least we corporate types know what it's like to work for a living."

"But what's the point if it kills you in the end? All work and no play, you know?" Surfer Boy took a sip of his beer. Even as he drank, there was a smirk hiding at the corner of his mouth.

Trevor wondered what the guy would do if he leaned over and kissed him there.

Jesus! He'd probably get decked or punched in the nuts. Clearly the man hadn't liked the fact Trevor had called a halt to their make-out session.

To redirect his mind from his horny thoughts, Trevor said, "I take it your personal philosophy is all play and no work?"

"I work. I just happen to work at something I love. There's a big difference."

Trevor turned to the man and assessed him. "What are you, the local beach guru?"

Surfer Boy raised a brow. "You learn a lot by watching people."

That was for sure. He'd pegged Trevor in a New York minute. It hadn't even taken half a second to assess him and cut it close to the bone.

"Since you already seem to have guessed so much about me, what do you do?"

"Besides philosophize? I'm a spelunker."

It took Trevor a moment or two to realize he meant he was a cave diver. That wasn't something most people did for a living. Could someone even make a living that way? Sounded kind of pointless. "So nothing to advance mankind."

"Does there need to be a higher purpose?" That same damn smile lodged in the corner of Surfer Boy's mouth. A sexy smile that fascinated and drew the eye. It beckoned and enticed a person to do something foolish like get involved.

"I think so." Trevor took a sip of his drink. "If there isn't, it is just empty work. Like cogs in a wheel spinning with no destination."

"That's a glass half-empty attitude."

Trevor shrugged. "It's the only one I've got."

"Give it time. Enough surf and sun down here and it will change anyone's attitude." Surfer Boy watched a couple across the dance floor. A silver fox moved with a woman who looked as if she was trying desperately to hold on to her youth. They were standing so close a piece of paper wouldn't fit between them.

A dark-haired local approached Surfer Boy. They fist bumped and then began to speak in rapid Spanish. Trevor only managed to pick up about one in every three words. It sounded as if they discussed people at the resort and something about a boat.

The newcomer glanced at Trevor and said something he didn't quite understand but that made Surfer Boy smile and… was that a blush under his tan?

Trevor grew warm. He glanced down into his drink and found his glass empty. He set it up on the bar and ordered another. Not that he wanted to get hammered, but he found he suddenly needed some fortification. Not to mention a bit of courage.

The local clapped Surfer Boy on the arm and then walked away.

Surfer Boy turned to Trevor. "Do you speak Spanish?"

Trevor met Surfer Boy's eyes. They were green with brilliant gold flecks around the pupils. He hadn't noticed that last night in the dim light. Gorgeous. The long dark lashes were out of place but made it all the harder to look away.

There was a moment of silence where time suspended. Surfer Boy let a slow, sexy smile fill his face. "Enjoy the rest of your vacation."

With that, he tipped his head and disappeared into the crowd.

Trevor sat there for a moment, wondering what had just happened and how in the hell he was going to find the guy in a resort the size of this one.

For the first time in years, Trevor felt alive. And sitting there in the middle of a bar thousands of miles away from home, he decided he liked the feeling.

CLIVE WENDED through the patrons on his way to the food. He was hungry, and the buffet was packed with all varieties of local seafood and vegetables. His stomach let out a growl. Concentration for food was hard to summon when his body craved something else.

Hookup was hotter than Santa Juanita at midday. Big dark eyes and short wavy hair that begged for hands to run through and mess it up. The body under the Henley looked as taut and firm as it had felt. The arms like steel bands. It was enough to make him crazy. God, he needed to get laid.

The best part? The cynical way Hookup looked at the world. It would be a challenge to show him that a little fun in the sun was just the prescription for corporate burnout.

And he was interested. It had been there in the depths of his dark eyes. Oh, he might want to play Mr. Hard-to-Get, but there was no doubt that eventually he'd turn into just Mr. Hard. And it had been hard.

Across the dance floor, Silver Fox was putting the moves on Orange Bikini. He was glad she'd taken his advice. Come to paradise with one person, explore all the riches and romance together, then leave with that person. It should have been a law.

He might have preferred variety in his own life, but if being in an open relationship hurt one of the people involved, it wasn't the one for them.

Clive picked up a huge shrimp and put it in his mouth as he made his way from the buffet to a table filled with his friends. They too lived near the resort and came in to work as guides or run the amusement concessions.

"Hey, look who showed up!" Marlie yelled to get the attention of the rest of the people at the table.

They all glanced up and said his name and then scooted over to make a place for him. He took the seat Phil had dragged over from another table and parked his butt.

"I'd like to thank the members of the tourism council for the warm welcome."

Everyone laughed and continued eating.

"So, who was that hunk at the bar you were talking to?" Juan Pablo scooped a big forkful of paella into his mouth and chewed.

"Didn't get his name. Uptight corporate type down here to chill and doesn't quite know how. Probably jonesing for his iPhone as we speak." Clive took some spiced meat and rolled it in a fresh tortilla with avocado slices. He wasn't about to tell his friends he'd damn near fucked the guy the night before. "I'd be willing to teach him."

They laughed again.

Marlie bumped his elbow. "I bet you would. How long has it been since you took on a tourist? Two, maybe three weeks. I think you've got some jonesing of your own going on."

His friends thought that was rather amusing. He failed to see the humor. If he didn't get laid soon, there wasn't going to be enough hand lotion on the island to pull him out of his miserable state.

It wasn't that he hadn't looked in every new batch of tourists who flooded the island. He just hadn't seen any he found attractive or interesting enough to take to bed. Well, other than Hookup, but that had been a dead end of sorts.

Clive might be just this side of a manwhore, but he did have his standards. It wasn't like he'd take anything with a swinging dick.

"I have an idea." Marlie rose from the table and hurried over to the bar.

Christ! She wasn't going over to bring Hookup to swim at the table with the local sharks was she? The poor boy really wasn't ready for that kind of indoctrination.

"Remind me to bury her in the sand later."

Juan Pablo and Carlos looked up from their plates. "She cares about you. You did a good thing getting her out of that bad relationship with Simon. She just wants to see you happy."

"By fixing me up with every dude I give a second look?" Clive tried not to peer in the direction of the bar, but it was hard. It took every ounce of his self-control to keep his mind focused on his dinner and not on what might be happening across the deck.

Carlos shrugged. His dark eyes were soft and gentle. "She's a romantic. She wants you to find a life partner."

The entire thought nearly put him off his dinner. He'd tried that route before and gotten seriously burned for the effort. He'd also gotten stabbed, gutted, speared, and walked on with cleats. His heart just wasn't into things like finding someone to spend the rest of his life with. He wasn't that guy. Maybe at one time, but that had been a long time ago.

He didn't want to go down that road again. It hurt too badly when illusions shattered and the real person was revealed. Simple, casual, hot with no strings attached, that's the way he preferred it.

He glanced out of the corner of his eye to check on Marlie. She and Hookup were having quite the little conversation. Dammit. If he didn't love her so much, he'd go over there and throttle her.

She'd been almost as big a mess as he'd been when she came to Santa Juanita. He'd already been an ex-pat for about four years when she'd shown up straight from Cali looking to start over. That was one of the draws of Santa Juanita—people came to the beautiful little South American island to make a new life.

When her crazyass boyfriend followed her down and started hassling and threatening her, Clive had put an abrupt stop to the torment. Simon had left the island and not bothered Marlie again.

Marlie returned and handed Clive a beer. She shimmied into her seat and smiled at him.

"I'm afraid to even ask."

"What? I only put a bug in his ear. Told him if he was interested in diving that he should check out the beach in the morning."

"Yeah. Thanks for that. I've never felt more like a high schooler in my life. Not even when I was one." Clive took a swig of the beer. Something told him it was a peace offering of sorts. "He knows I'm into spelunking."

"Oh, you managed to get around to announcing that, but you didn't get his name? Classic Clive there."

"I prefer a bit of mystery. It adds to the chase." He took another bite of his dinner. Heady anticipation moved through him. Oh, he was definitely going to chase the guy, but subtly, so Hookup didn't realize he was being pursued.

"So you don't want to know his name?"

"No. I'll get it myself. I still might be able to salvage a bit of my cool." Not to mention he wouldn't have to admit to his friends he'd already been told the name and promptly forgotten it in the heat of a rather intense bout of make-out magic.

The music changed around them. The beat ratcheted up a few notches. The bass made its way in a serpentine through his body. He loved Latin music. Loved the passion and freedom of the beat. The general love of life that poured from every note. It was as hot and intense as the people who embraced it.

He wanted to dance. Coolness kept him in his seat. The only person he wanted to dance with at the moment was tucked up to the bar, pretending he wasn't in the middle of a party. The only rhythm Clive wanted to move to was one very private and intimate.

Chapter Three

ALL NIGHT long, contracts and projects haunted Trevor's dreams. They called to him like lost children in need of a parent. He woke in a cold sweat and reached for his phone. No calls.

How could the damn company have made it four days without him? Four days he'd been on this godforsaken rock of an island, and he'd yet to get word from the home office. Was his exile so complete that even his friends at the office had forgotten about him?

Maybe his e-mail account was down? The server might be having problems and not forwarding the appropriate e-mails to him. He'd have to send a text to someone and find out.

In the meantime, it wouldn't hurt to hit the beach. Luckily his mother's side of the family was Italian, and his "pale skin" had started to turn to a nice deep olive in the sun. He still slathered on a handful of sunblock before going outdoors. It was the prudent thing to do.

As he worked the lotion over his shoulders, a face came into his mind as crystal clear as the water around the cove. Surfer Boy had been haunting him for days. Something about those eyes was enough to spear a person through.

Trevor had seen Surfer Boy around the marina and at the cove. If the guy was here to do some serious cave diving, then he'd come to the right place. All the little rocky outcroppings around the island hid some very deep and unfriendly areas. He'd looked at the maps of all the places to dive close to the resort. There was even the wreck of an old Spanish galleon four miles offshore.

No doubt the dude wanted to see everything there was to see before leaving for home—wherever that might be. He'd not really given any information in the bar. His eyes had been full of mystery. Each time he'd spotted Surfer Boy since that night he'd been in the company of a group. Not exactly the best situation for approaching the guy. Besides, what was he supposed to say? *Hey dude, surf's up in my pants.*

It had been years since he'd been on a dive. Almost a lifetime ago. When he was in college and had his entire life ahead of him and the future was bright and shiny. Back when he was still content to live in the moment. Back when Jason was alive.

He threw a shirt on over his shorts and headed for the door. Maybe he'd walk down to the marina and see if he could rent some dive equipment. It was something to do anyway.

Being exiled in paradise was only fun if there was someone to share the experience. He was often at loose ends. None of the island's many pleasures appealed to him. Nothing seemed to matter. What was the use of being down here taking a damned vacation when he had so many projects and patents to work on in New Jersey?

He went down to the lobby and checked his phone again. Nothing. Weird. He could have sworn he'd felt it vibrate.

"Good morning, Mr. Donohue." The desk clerk waved at him as he crossed the lobby and headed for the door leading out to the marina.

Maria had been very friendly and attentive since his arrival. He hated to burst her bubble by giving her the facts of his life. The way she smiled and batted her long black lashes at him, he had the feeling she wanted more than just a *good morning* in return.

The sun was full up and cast an unmerciful heat on the island. The sand had already gotten so hot he was at risk of losing a couple layers of skin. Thank God, he'd worn shoes.

A boat had just pulled into the marina. Surfer Boy jumped over the side and helped to secure the craft to the dock. Sweat glistened on his golden skin. Every cut of muscle shone to perfection. He turned and picked up a bag he'd thrown on the dock, giving Trevor a flash of smooth tawny hair.

Trevor's mouth went dry. Damn, the guy was good enough to eat and was obviously a local. No wonder he acted like he owned the beach.

He tracked Surfer Boy's movements down the dock and up to the sidewalk at the water's edge. The closer he came, the more Trevor's feet refused to move.

Surfer Boy gave a little nod as he walked by, but otherwise he didn't say anything. Trevor stood there for a few moments wondering what to do next. Obviously he had a hard time approaching the guy when he was alone as well as with a group.

He was getting nowhere fast.

If there was anyone who knew how to live in the moment, it was that guy. Not that Trevor wanted to learn. He just didn't want to die of boredom on this rock.

He continued on down to the marina office. Office was a misnomer—the place was little more than a stucco shed with a counter between the attendant and the customer. How was that efficient or even a good business setup for something like a rental office?

"May I help you?" The agent spoke in lightly accented English. Trevor had not been surprised that the high-end resort employed people who were at least bilingual. In some instances he'd heard a few of them speaking French, German, Italian, and Portuguese to other tourists. This was not a poor man's retreat by any stretch of the imagination. Whoever ran the resort knew how to accommodate the tourists to make and keep them happy.

"I need information on local diving." Trevor put up his hand. "I have been dive certified, but it's been a very long time. I'll need a refresher of sorts."

"Do you have a C-card?"

He doubted it, but he took his wallet out and fished around for one. Surprise of a lifetime, there it was, stuck behind an old receipt for gasoline and his library card. "Here."

The attendant looked at the card and the date on it. "How long has it been since you were on a dive?"

"About eight years."

"You'll need the turbo refresher."

Oh, that did not sound good. It had the ring of being submerged in a shark tank during a hurricane.

"Can I get it done in one afternoon?"

"I'll let the divemaster decide." The attendant typed something into a computer and pulled it up on screen. "Clive is here in the morning. He's the best."

Clive the diver? What kind of weird Dr. Seuss world was this that the man's name and profession rhymed? It was wrong on every level.

Trevor gave the attendant an unsure smile. "Do I need to sign up for the class or make an appointment?"

"Oh, yeah. He's a very popular instructor. It's best to make a reservation."

Trevor did so and paid in advance for the class, then went back up to the resort in search of something to do before he went insane. He checked his phone. Still no call from home.

Had everyone on the planet forgotten he was alive? They said absence made the heart grow fonder, but in this case, the heart just completely forgot.

Hell, his mother hadn't even called him. That wasn't a good sign. She must have talked to Geoff about the reason for the vacation. Not that he allowed his mother to make decisions for him, but the words "concerned," "unhealthy," and "obsessive" had been bandied around a bit too much lately with Trevor as the subject.

Talk about making a guy feel special. He'd poured his heart and soul into Global. After the shooting, it was the only thing he'd had to hold on to, the rope that had pulled him from the abyss when his life had turned to shit. If he lost his position there…. Well, he wasn't even going to think about it. He'd lost the most important thing in the world to him once already, and he'd survived. A job he'd find. It would suck, but he'd find one.

A screen in the lobby displayed local happenings. The village down the road was having a street fair. Maybe he'd go over and check it out, drink some tequila and try to remember what he'd loved most when he was younger, before life and work consumed his thoughts. Before all his dreams had a hole blown through them and he'd buried himself in work to forget the pain.

"You look like you're at a loose end."

The deep voice moved over Trevor in a sensual wave. He turned and fell headlong into Surfer Boy's green eyes. The dude wasn't alone. A bright blue parrot with a yellow mask and breast sat perched on his shoulder.

The bird whistled. It bobbed its head up and down. *"Fuck me, sailor."*

Surfer Boy's face went red. "Rodger. Mind your manners."

Trevor was stunned. He didn't know quite what to say to the man or his profane bird.

"We were just heading to the street fair in Poco Carlita if you're interested." Surfer Boy turned and started walking toward the lobby door.

Trevor glanced around. Other than the bird, the guy was alone, and it was an invitation, right? He caught up at the door and fell in step beside him as they crossed the parking lot.

"Are you going to walk to the village?"

"Sure. It's not that far. Besides, Rodger likes to feel the wind in his feathers. Right, buddy?" Surfer Boy reached up and scratched the bird, who let out a sound of pleasure.

Lucky-ass bird.

"Aren't you afraid to take him into public? He might get you arrested."

Surfer Boy laughed. "I doubt that. The locals know him."

"Does he belong to the resort?" It seemed a sensible question.

"No. He's mine."

It figured an unconventional person would have a pet that wasn't the standard dog or cat.

They walked along a path that cut through the tree line and ended at a dirt road. Music came from the center of town, as did shouts of laughter. The scent of fragrant spices filled the air, making Trevor's mouth water. He'd not eaten anything that morning, and the noise from his belly was starting to get embarrassing.

Surfer Boy looked over at Trevor and gave him that sexy, dick-hardening smile. "You should take advantage of morning room service."

Trevor had a hard time keeping his mind on where he stepped. Why did everything out of Surfer Boy's mouth sound like a proposition? Did he do that on purpose? And what would Surfer Boy do if Trevor said something just as leading in return? Probably swallow his tongue.

"Look, about the other night—"

Surfer Boy held up his hand and stalled the apology before Trevor had a chance to make it. "Don't bother. You decided you weren't interested after all. It happens." He cast a puzzled look at Trevor. "Never to me, mind you, but it happens."

Trevor swallowed and felt his pride slide down his throat. "You're wrong. I *was* interested. Very much so. It's just been a really long time."

The tone of his voice made Surfer Boy stop. Rodger's wings lifted a bit. One came up higher than the other in a crazy lopsided dance. Surfer Boy reached up to calm the bird, his penetrating gaze never leaving Trevor's face.

"If you swing my way, that's cool. But I really draw the line at men who come down here to get their down low on and then go home after a great fuck, viewing me as their dirty secret. I'm out and proud of it. If you're not, then I can't help you with it." Surfer Boy turned and started walking down the path that led to the village.

Trevor shoved his hands in his pockets and shook his head. Surfer Boy was very sensitive to rejection. He started to call out after him, but the small issue of not knowing Surfer Boy's real name surfaced.

"Jesus." He rolled his eyes and jogged to catch up. "Look, don't walk away with the wrong idea. I did want you. *Do* want you. I have no qualms about being who and what I am. I came out a long time ago and live my life accordingly."

It just hadn't gone the way he'd planned. The familiar twinges of failure, loss, and guilt pinched him under the ribs. He winced.

Surfer Boy gave a nod. "Good to know."

All right. What exactly did that mean? This guy was just too smooth, too in control. He seemed to flow through life like a lazy river. Him and his bird.

Trevor held out his hand. "Truce?"

Surfer Boy took his hand. "We were never at war. I make it a point not to fight. Too much energy expended that could be used for other things."

And there it was again, that sexy glint in his eyes that said he'd rather bend Trevor over and fuck him stupid than talk to him.

Everything inside Trevor went hot and tight. It was a little flattering and a lot disorienting. Briefly he wondered how many times Surfer Boy had been down this road. Well, not the road they were on, but the one that led to a hot night in sweaty sheets with a near stranger.

The man was too intense in a laid-back kind of way. If that was even possible. He was like some kind of sexual missile. If Trevor didn't keep his radar up, it was going to be a direct hit with total annihilation.

Surfer Boy turned and cut through a break in the trees. "Are you coming?"

Trevor let out a breath and took the plunge. God, he hoped so.

Chapter Four

THE STREET fair was in full swing. Judging from the smells, Paolo and Maria-Sophia were at it with the huge cauldron of spiced meat. Clive took in a deep breath and let the aroma coat his tongue and palate.

He held the foliage back so Hookup could step through into the town proper. Nothing like taking the shortcut to the village. The hidden route was much quicker and afforded privacy where the main road was filled with tourists and locals. He'd wanted a few moments alone with Hookup. There had been times over the last few days when Clive had felt as if he was being watched, only to turn and see the Roman god staring from the distance.

Clive tried not to think about the heat burning him from head to foot. Coming to the street fair was a way to get Hookup away from the resort and see him in a more neutral setting. Maybe the guy would loosen up a bit. It couldn't hurt.

The poor dude needed to relax in the worst way. A blow job would probably go a long way to creating a thorough attitude adjustment.

Hookup stepped through the foliage and laughed. "Wow. It looks like something out of a movie set."

The town barely had a name. The locals called it simply the village. Maps called it Poco Carlita. It had started as a small farming community that supplied food to the larger city of Cartajuan about six miles to the south of the resort. The town had spread out to include about a dozen streets but still had no streetlights or motor traffic.

Music swelled from a small stage set up at the end of the street where a local band played contemporary Latin dance hits as well as folk music. Handmade textiles were offered for sale at kiosks. Games and competitions were ongoing at the west side of the town. Once the sun set, the lanterns strung across would be lit and give the square a romantic flair. Clive knew. He'd been to street fairs a few times over the years.

The one last year had ended with him winning first place in a local wrestling competition and then screwing the hell out of the runner-up. It had been an awesome day and night all around.

Hookup wandered over to a food stand. Fragrant steam rose from a large metal pan filled with ground meat. "I need something to eat."

Clive followed him over to the stand. Paolo raised his hand as he stirred the simmering meat with the other. "Hey. Haven't seen you in a while."

It was said in rapid-fire Spanish. Clive answered in like form. "Been busy taking the tourists out to the galleon. It's a good season."

Paolo nodded. "We've benefited from the extra trade."

It showed. The houses and other buildings looked freshly painted and roofed. Prosperity had finally come to the village.

Paolo jerked his head in Hookup's direction. "Who's your friend?"

"Tourist from the resort."

Paolo smiled. Maria-Sophia entered the stand from the back, carrying a clay bowl of fresh-pressed tortillas.

They greeted each other, and she stuck her hand in her pocket and pulled out a few nuts. "I stocked my pocket in case you brought Rodger."

She handed the parrot a nut.

"Damn time," Rodger said by way of a thank you.

"Can I get your friend something?" Maria-Sophia waited expectantly to serve the men food.

Clive tapped Hookup with his bent knuckle. "She wants to know if you want anything."

Hookup rubbed his stomach. "It all looks good."

Clive ordered for both of them and handed Maria-Sophia enough for both meals and then some. They were good, hardworking people who had treated him like a son since he'd met them shortly after moving to the island.

He handed Hookup a plate and then said his good-byes. Rodger danced on his shoulder as the beat of the music became more frenetic.

"Hold still, buddy. You'll make me drop my lunch."

"Tastes like shit."

Hookup walked beside him as they wended through the stalls that displayed a wide array of local gifts and trinkets.

"This is a good place to stock up on souvenirs." Clive pointed to a pair of statues representing the Day of the Dead.

Hookup blanched. "Not my thing. They just look like bad luck."

"Actually they're good luck." Clive took a bite of his lunch. "There are also plenty of handmade clay pots, pitchers, and plates. Some of the artwork on them is beautiful."

"I really didn't come down here to take a bunch of shit back home with me. As a matter of fact, I hadn't even thought about taking anything back." Hookup wandered to the counter and picked up a large platter painted in a mosaic of blues, purples, and stark white. "How would I get something like this back to the States? It'd break in my luggage."

"You're a fatalist." Clive moved on to another stand. This one had handblown glass spheres. Nothing useful, but decorative.

"I'm a realist. You've been through customs lately?"

Clive shook his head. "I haven't left the island in ten years, except to go to the mainland."

"Not even to go back home? Don't you miss it?"

No, Clive most certainly didn't miss it, and he wasn't going to get into the why of it with Hookup. "Not really."

"You've completely gone the expat expressway, haven't you?"

"I suppose so, but it works for me. I love it down here and don't have any plans to leave anytime soon. Why should I? I've got everything I need. Good friends, good food, a job I love without any of the hassles that come with quote civilization." The glass globes seemed tacky and tarnished now. Clive stepped away from the stand and found a place to sit on a sizable boulder to eat his meal.

Hookup sat at an adjacent angle, facing away from him.

"Why did you come down here?" Clive wished he could see Hookup's face, but short of craning his neck around, he had no way to see him from his position.

Hookup stopped with his fork halfway to his mouth. "Forced vacation."

Clive shook his head in pity. "Forced? Someone had to force you to come down here? Wow. Most people are dying to get away from the rat race, and you wanted to stay in the middle of the maze without ever finding the cheese."

"It's not quite that pathetic." Hookup glanced over his shoulder at Clive before going back to his meal. "My boss thought I was heading toward what he called *manic burnout*."

Clive laughed. "What the hell is that? Some kind of psychobabble diagnosis he came up with on his own?"

"Pretty much." Hookup made a half turn to face Clive. His expression was one of sorrow and confusion, as if he had no idea if this vacation was the last hurrah before the unemployment line or firing squad. "I'm a workaholic. He told me if I kept going at it like I am, I'd be dead before I'm forty."

"Is your boss a doctor?"

Red crept up Hookup's cheeks and exploded across his face. "As a matter of fact he is. So am I, for that matter, though I haven't practiced in a long time."

Clive made a face. "You're a doctor? As in medical doctor?"

Hookup's brow furrowed in annoyance. "Yes. Is that so hard to believe?"

Clive shrugged and dug back into his meal. "Not at all. It just seems odd that you'd spend all that time on education and residency, if you didn't intend to practice once you finished."

Hookup's expression grew sour. "It's nothing I want to talk about now."

Rodger flapped his wings. *"You're a fucking wimp bastard!"*

Hookup scoffed. "Even your bird has contempt for me."

"Rodger has contempt for everyone. It's part of his charm." Clive dug into his pocket and held a sunflower seed up for the bird. Rodger daintily plucked the offering from Clive's fingers.

"I bet he doesn't talk to you like that."

"You'd lose. He calls me a *stupid fucker* most of the time."

Hookup laughed. The sound was deep, rich, and made of hotness. It lodged in Clive's balls in an unexpected and erotic way.

"Maybe he thinks it's a term of endearment."

"I don't know what he thinks, but he's got a worse mouth than a sailor on shore leave." A decided crack of shell crunched close to his ear as if in punctuation of Rodger's poor manners.

"Have you tried teaching him alternate phrases?"

"Are you kidding? It would completely ruin his groove. He just wouldn't be Jolly Rodger, then."

Hookup gave a kind of lopsided grin as the wind ruffled his hair. His dark eyes sparkled, and Clive was a goner. There was something different about this guy. Something he just couldn't put his finger on. And for the first time in a long time, Clive wanted to explore what it meant to be so drawn to another person. Not just for sex, but for other, deeper reasons.

Hookup had a story he wasn't willing to tell. That was fine. Clive didn't want to tell his much either—not at the moment.

His throat tightened. It was hard to choke down his food. Warning signals went off in his brain. Maybe inviting Hookup along for the day had been a bad idea. Seeing him begin to relax and enjoy himself was a dangerous thing.

"So do you have a boyfriend back home?" Clive heard himself ask, but had not given his brain or mouth the command to do so.

"No. Only work. It's my master and commander. Both religion and salvation." Hookup placed his hand on his heart in feigned reverence. "I give all I am to the corporate gods."

"Is it any wonder, then, you were forced to come down here?" Clive stood. His plate was empty and belly full. "Come on, let's walk around and see what we can see."

Hookup followed suit.

They threw their plates into the trash receptacle and ambled down the main street. Every few steps or so someone would shout a hello and wave. He waved back as Rodger flapped a wing in greeting.

"You know everyone in this town." Hookup glanced around at the throngs of people who all smiled and beckoned for them to come to their stands. "Are you the mayor or something?"

"We'll go with 'or something.'" Clive gave Hookup a sly smile. It was best to keep him guessing. Too much information and he'd risk the chance of getting close. He didn't want to get close. At the end of his vacation, forced or not, Hookup was going to leave and head back to the altar of his corporate religion.

Clive herded Hookup west and to the end of the street, where feats of strength and endurance were being played out by men wearing little more than flaps of fabric held together by two strings tied at the sides. The combatants were slicked up with oil, making their skin glow a dark bronze under the unforgiving sun. One wore blue paint on his face; the other wore red.

The two opponents circled each other, hands up and legs bent into a crouch as if about to spring into action. A chalk circle marked the out-of-bounds area. Blue lunged, grabbing Red by the shoulders and forcing him back to the line. Red dug into the ground, his bare feet gaining traction on the dirt. Strong leg muscles bunched. He shoved Blue back three feet, all the way to the center.

Cheers went up around the huddled spectators. Shouts of encouragement for both men peppered the air. Money changed hands as bets were placed.

"What a stud!" Rodger called to the opponents.

Clive chuckled and reached up to scratch the silly bird.

Hookup stared at Rodger. "It's eerie how appropriately inappropriate he is."

"You don't know the half of it." Clive winked. "At first I thought it was a coincidence. Now I'm not really sure. He's very perceptive."

Red grabbed Blue around the torso and forced him to the ground. Limbs slipped and slid over each other. Loincloths flapped, giving the crowd a perfect view of their male equipage.

Hookup nodded in the direction of their bared essentials. "I'd think the risk of injury outstrips the need to prove strength in this case."

Clive frowned. "No. That's part of the draw. Only a real man would dare to wrestle with his masculinity so exposed."

Hookup raised a brow. "You sound like you approve."

One of the locals, Guillermo, who often helped Clive on his boat, shuffled up to Clive, holding out a loincloth and nodding in encouragement.

Clive held up his hands in a respectful decline and shook his head. He switched to Spanish. "No. No. I'm only a spectator this year."

Hookup watched the exchange with narrowed eyes as if concentrating to try to get the gist of the conversation.

Guillermo continued to nod. "You are the champion. You have to compete. It is the tradition. All these people came to see you put the challenger down."

The corner of Clive's mouth lifted in a naughty smile. "All right." He bowed slightly. "I honor your traditions."

Guillermo thrust the loincloth into Clive's hands and turned away, shouting to the crowd that the champion had accepted the challenge. A cheer went up around the spectators as they turned to Clive as one.

Hookup gazed at Clive as if he'd lost his mind. "You can't be serious."

"It's their tradition, and as a local I have to honor them or I set myself apart. These people have been very good to me since I moved here. If they want me to prove my strength, I will."

"But why you?"

Clive gave Hookup a heated look. "You want to join me in the ring and see for yourself?"

Pink exploded across Hookup's cheeks and in the V of his shirt. "No, thank you. You'll have to do this one alone. But I will hold Rodger for you."

Clive put up his hand and transferred Rodger from his shoulder. "Hey, buddy. Want to sit on his shoulder for a while?"

Rodger bobbed and danced, spreading his lopsided wings. *"Hot damn!"*

"That's as good as a yes." The bird shuffled a bit before settling, and immediately began to pick at Hookup's hair.

"He's not going to bite me, is he?"

"This is his affectionate side. He likes you a lot." That made two of them.

"Okay. As long as you don't come back and I'm missing an ear."

Clive kicked off his shoes, then began to unbutton his shorts.

"What are you doing?" Hookup's eyes were rounded with scandal.

"Getting into my loincloth. What does it look like I'm doing?"

"You can't change out here." Hookup glanced around at the crowds of milling people.

Clive was mystified by Hookup's prudishness. "Why not? What difference does it make if I change out here or behind a rock? People are still going to see my junk when I get in the ring."

"Maybe so, but in there"—Hookup gestured toward the ring— "it's expected. Out here is just showing off."

Clive laughed. He couldn't help himself. It was one of the funniest things he'd ever heard. "You did say you're a trained physician, right?"

"Well, yes."

"And by that I'm assuming you have seen naked bodies before, right?"

"Yes."

"Then where does this modesty come from? For fuck's sake, you're supposed to be on vacation enjoying yourself. Leave all your hang-ups in the airport, but don't bring them to the island." Clive shoved his shorts down his legs and stepped out of them, then removed his shirt. He tied the loincloth around his waist while watching Hookup, who had turned away from the scene with a face blazing as bright as a Santa Juanita sunset.

"You can look at me now. I'm dressed."

Hookup pointed in the general direction of the loincloth. "*That* is not dressed."

Clive stepped into Hookup's personal space so their mouths were only inches apart. "This from the man who nearly got himself fucked stupid on the first night here?"

Hookup's gaze landed squarely on Clive's mouth. "That was different. We were alone. It was dark."

"Oh, so you like it in the dark? Maybe I'll make it my mission while you're here to show you the pleasures found in the sunlight."

Hookup made a sound in the back of his throat. "You're incorrigible."

"I think the word you're looking for is *encouraging*." Clive leaned forward and took in a deep breath of spices and sandalwood mixed with the scent of peppers. "Maybe even irresistible."

"Oh, you're definitely that," Hookup agreed.

Cheers went up from the ring. Money was distributed to the winners. Red stood victorious as Blue picked himself up from the ground and dusted dirt from his sticky, oiled form.

Hookup had his hands on his hips. "He looks like a powdered donut."

"You still hungry?" Clive took the jar of oil the official handed him. He thrust it at Hookup. "Here, slick me up."

"What?"

"You heard me. I need to be oiled. It's part of the rules." Clive stuck his chest out, seeing if Hookup would do it for him. The rules did not prohibit a combatant from oiling the areas of their body within their reach, only their backs. However, it was so much better to watch Hookup squirm with indecision.

Finally he grabbed the bottle with something close to violence and squirted a large handful into his palm. He slapped it on Clive's chest with a crack of skin, causing several people to turn and snicker.

"Careful. You don't want to mark the champion before he goes into the ring. It's considered bad form."

Hookup's gaze collided with Clive's. "Champion? You're the champion?"

"You seem surprised." Christ on a bicycle, it was hard to keep a straight face.

"I probably shouldn't be." Hookup slid his hand across Clive's pecs, his gaze fixated on the movement of his hand across Clive's skin.

The touch was both electrifying and erotic. All right, so the bastard had turned the tables on him without even realizing it. Clive's cock began to stir.

"That's enough. Do my back and I'll work on the front."

Was that a laugh he heard as he turned around? It was Clive's turn to grow a few shades redder. Damn. Caught in his own trap. How embarrassing.

So now he stood in the middle of the village with the makings of an impressive erection. He closed his eyes and began to silently recite the tide table as Hookup took his sweet time oiling up Clive's shoulders and lower back.

"That's good enough. My challenger is waiting." Clive stepped away and approached Guillermo.

"Are you ready?"

"I can take him," Clive assured his friend. "Paint me."

Guillermo dipped his fingers into the gold paint and smeared a line across each of Clive's cheeks. Gold was restricted for use only by the reigning champion. If Clive lost the match, the gold would be taken off and replaced by silver. It was a bit of a hierarchy to those who competed and let all who saw them for the rest of the day know who had prevailed in the games.

Clive stepped into the ring.

His challenger was the winner of the last match. Red looked at him with blood in his eyes. This man wanted to win and was going to prove himself the best no matter what. Well, Clive had a thing or two to say about that. He was not about to get his ass kicked in front of Hookup during a festival. Not going to happen.

Clive sized up Red. The man was solid, stocky. His reach wasn't near the length of Clive's, which put Red at a disadvantage. However, he was also about four to five inches shorter as well, which meant he'd be good at sliding under Clive's arms and getting a lock around his waist in order to take him down.

There was something familiar in that stance and glare. Shit, had he beaten this guy last year? Man, did he hate grudge matches.

The official blew a whistle and the match began.

Clive circled, never taking his gaze from Red's. If an opponent was going to make a move, Clive could see it in their eyes first. It had always been that way.

He'd wrestled Greco-Roman style in high school and college. This wasn't much different as far as moves allowed. He used his experience to his advantage and forced Red to make the first move. It was a mistake Red knew he'd made as soon as he'd done so.

Clive locked his arms around Red's waist and took him to the ground in one fell swoop. The crowd sucked in a collective breath. Red bowed his back upward to keep his shoulders from touching the dirt.

Clive lost his grip on the slippery skin, and Red turned quickly, coming up behind him. Strong arms clamped around Clive's torso and swung him around, but Clive flipped at the last second and took the top position.

Red was strong, he'd give him that. He was heavy with dense muscles, which made for a very worthy opponent. Though Clive knew most of the men around the village, he'd never met this particular one, outside of thinking he knew him from the previous year's competition. He must have come from one of the outlying farms to participate in the games. Sure was built like a fucking ox.

The Red-painted devil slipped away again, but Clive used the momentum of the turn against him and brought him to the ground a third time.

Cheers were flowing, changing the energy of the arena. From the corner of his eye, he caught the vague image of a bright blue parrot on the shoulder of a dark god, and strength surged through him.

He pinned Red to the ground, and the official blew the whistle to end the match. Clive rose and held his hand out for his opponent, who batted his hand away.

"Sore loser." Clive didn't even bother to revert to Spanish. Red would know the sentiment by the way the words were said.

The official dressed Red down for his behavior. Red glared at Clive as if it were all his fault. Childish behavior in a grown man was so unbecoming.

Clive turned and started to walk away, but shouts erupted behind him. He pivoted just in time to get shoved across the ring to the other side as Red came at him in a fury.

Without rules, the man didn't stand a chance.

Clive pushed Red away as Red swung out. Clive ducked to the right and came up with a left hook. Red's head snapped back, and he hit the ground, out cold.

Red's friends rushed forward. Clive pointed at him.

"His behavior is inexcusable and an embarrassment to the community. Wake him up and take him home."

The men nodded as if afraid to argue. It was in their best interest not to. Clive scanned the crowd who'd remained, and they were not pleased with Red's conduct. It soured what should have been a friendly competition. The man would be stripped of his right to wear the second-place silver paint for the rest of the festival. He'd earned no bragging rights or made any friends. The villagers took their traditions seriously. Red would find out just how much when he woke up.

Clive accepted congratulations from the crowd and accolades for putting Red in his place. He hated to burst their bubbles by telling them it was self-defense more than outrage that had him swinging fists, but let them think what they liked.

The festival had lost its appeal.

He was going to change out of the loincloth and back into his clothes and go home. There was no reason to stay around here any longer. He glanced at Hookup.

Hookup's dark eyes were full of concern and a host of questions. Clive looked away as he grabbed for his clothes. "Give me a few minutes and we can go."

"You really want to leave because some asshole decided to take an unsportsmanlike swipe at you?"

Clive gave Hookup a look that had sent most men cowering. It had no effect on Dr. Tourist.

"I would have thought you were made of tougher stuff than that."

It was a goad that Clive wanted to acknowledge, but stubbornness made him ignore it.

Clive tore off the loincloth and stepped into his shorts. "Let's pretend for a moment that you know me even a little. Why is hanging around a fair where I've become a disruption to the festivities a good idea?"

Hookup glanced around, then back at Clive. "Oh, I don't know, maybe because his actions aren't a reflection on you or anything you did. To stay here and show the village that just because your opponent acted like a middle school bully that you're above it."

Clive pulled his shirt on. "Contrary to what you might think of me, I don't like violence. Tests of strength, endurance, and skill, fine. Brutality for brutality's sake I can do without."

Hookup's shoulders came down as he let out a sigh. "And those here who know you will understand."

"Not if I strut around here like cock of the walk."

Hookup's eyes dilated and his gaze dropped to Clive's fly. A sidewise smile curled his mouth so deliciously up at the corner. "You already have, my friend."

The comment had the desired effect. The intense moment dissipated, replaced by one of scorching heat and remembered passion.

Clive took a step closer to Hookup while buttoning his shirt. "Tell me you didn't enjoy it just a little bit."

Hookup's color deepened. "More than a little. You're one sexy bastard, I'll give you that."

Clive laughed, further lightening his mood. Promise for a good day buzzed on the air. Who knew what they might get into after dark fell and all the shadows grew long, concealing private places perfect for a little outdoor sex.

Wait, this was Hookup he was with—they'd get things going and the man would pull back like a virgin on a first date. In other words, Clive wasn't going to hold his breath that the promise he saw in

Hookup's eyes might lead anywhere but disappointment. Clive wasn't going to count his cocks before they hatched.

He held out his hand for Rodger. The parrot shuffled on Hookup's shoulder, moving closer to his head. "You want to stay there?"

"Hot damn!"

"You don't mind if he uses you for a perch awhile longer, do you?" Never let it be said that Clive thrust his bird where it wasn't wanted.

"No. He's fine. I kind of like his weight on my shoulder. I'm feeling all piratey."

"I'm not sure that's a word, but knock yourself out."

They took off in no particular direction through town. There were more vendors and games. At the far end of town someone had set up a course for throwing javelins and targets for archery.

"Do you want to try either of those?"

Hookup shook his head at the javelins. "I've never thrown one of those before. I have tried archery—I can at least hit the target."

Clive dug into his pocket and pulled out some coins. "Here, give these to the big guy over there. He'll set you up with equipment."

Hookup put his hand up to refuse the money. "I can pay for my own. You already bought me lunch."

"Well, consider it thanks for holding Rodger while I made good on my obligation." Clive took Hookup's hand in his and plunked the money down. Instant current ran over Clive's fingers and up his arms. He cupped Hookup's hand in his and brushed their thumbs together. "So thanks."

Hookup made a sound in the back of his throat. "You make it really hard to be good in public."

"Or really good to be hard."

"I'm going to go shoot a target and get my mind off that image." He reached up and petted Rodger's head. "I'm going to give you back to your daddy now."

Clive raised a brow at the "daddy" reference. "I'm more his *amigo* than his daddy."

"Stick 'em up, gringo!" Rodger squawked as he ruffled his feathers and beat his wings, transferring to Clive's shoulder.

Hookup looked startled. "Where did that come from?"

"He's addicted to old spaghetti westerns. I shouldn't encourage him, but it keeps him entertained." Clive scratched Rodger's crown. "You want to go watch the archery?"

"He-Man. Masters of the Universe."

Clive laughed. "I don't know where that one came from. Honest."

"Sure. I bet you don't." Hookup gave his money to Raul, the attendant working the archery event.

Raul gave a nod of greeting to Clive and handed Hookup a bow and quiver of arrows.

"Tres."

"You're at the third target."

Hookup looked over his shoulder at Clive. "Yeah, I got that. My Spanish might be a little rusty, but I can pick up some words."

"I just wanted to make sure you get to the right spot." Clive followed in step behind Hookup. "Didn't want you piercing someone else's target."

"If I don't hit my own, I guarantee I won't hit anyone else's either." This was said as Hookup walked up to the line and lifted the bow to test the tension. "Wow. This thing might look like a relic, but it's strong as fuck."

Clive affected a considering pose. "And exactly how strong would that be?"

"Pretty strong."

Clive smiled. At least Hookup was loosening up a bit. For a while there, he'd worried the situation might be worse than he'd first thought. After a few shots of tequila and some of Raul's homemade *cerveza,* Clive was sure Hookup would be loose as a goose. He didn't know many men who could withstand the double down effect of Raul's *cerveza* as a tequila chaser. It had put many a stout man under the table, including Clive on more than one occasion.

Hookup notched an arrow and pulled the string. He waited a beat or two and let go without moving anything more than his fingers. Watching him was pure poetry.

The arrow flew and landed on the target, slightly below the bull's-eye, solidly in the red.

Hookup looked at the bow, made a face, and notched a second arrow. This one hit closer to the eye, right on the edge of yellow and red, above the center.

He held up a finger, then adjusted his stance and stepped back about a foot. The third arrow hit dead center. Hookup turned and smiled. "Pretty good, considering I haven't done this in about eight years."

"I'd say that's excellent under the circumstances."

Hookup faced the target again and shot his last two arrows. Both hit the lower yellow ring. He smiled and took out his phone and snapped a picture of the target.

"You want to go again?" Clive made the offer as casually as possible, though seeing the happy smile on Hookup's handsome face made Clive's throat want to close with emotion.

What was it about this guy that got to him?

On looks he was hot, and his body was rock-hard and to die for, but socially and philosophically they couldn't be more different. But then this wasn't anything permanent. It was a vacation fling for Hookup. For Clive it was a means to getting laid. Nothing more, nothing less.

Hookup reached into his pocket and pulled out some coins. "Yes, but let me buy my own arrows this time."

"Whatever."

Clive took the money and headed back to Raul. He switched to Spanish. "Five more, please."

"Your friend is a decent shot."

"He hit the target, which is a sight more than I could have done."

Raul pointed at the gold paint still on Clive's face. "Yes, but you show your strength and skill in other ways."

"I suppose I do." Clive took a chance that Raul may have heard about the commotion down at the ring. "Do you know the guy who pulled the red paint this year?"

Raul shook his head. "Whoever he is, he'll not be here long. The farmers won't like a troublemaker working their land."

That was an understatement. Men who worked for the farmers did so for long hours in close proximity. Any little ripple of dissent could be felt throughout the entire organization. Landowners on Santa Juanita didn't mistreat their employees, as there were few enough of them to go around. Most of the locals worked for the resorts, earning a better paycheck than they could as unskilled farm labor. Therefore, the landowners had to pay a competitive wage or risk losing workers to the resort or mainland.

"If you hear anything, send me word at the resort."

"Will do."

Clive took the second quiver and headed back to Hookup. An uneasy feeling settled over him. Someone had to know Red. He wouldn't have gotten into the competition without someone vouching for him.

"Here." Clive handed the arrows to Hookup.

"What's the matter?"

"Nothing. Local situation. Nothing important." Clive waved a hand in the direction of the target. "Come on, show-off, let's see how good you do this time."

Hookup managed to strike all the arrows in the yellow zone, but none dead center. He lifted a shoulder. "Not bad, but not champion material either."

Clive tried for humble. It didn't work. "We can't all be champions."

"No. I suppose we can't." Hookup smiled broadly and pointed at the target. A dimple indented into a deep mark on his cheek. "But that was some awesome shooting. You have to give me that."

Christ, Clive was a goner for a dimple. "I'll give it to you."

"What do I do with the arrows?"

"Leave them. Take the bow back to Raul. He'll have people clear the targets when he calls a break in the shooting."

They walked back to the vendor stand, and Hookup handed over the bow with a nod of thanks. "Where did you want to go to now?"

Clive stretched out a hand. "I can show you some more of the island if you want."

"Sure. It might help me get myself acclimated better."

Only a corporate type would use the word *acclimate* while on vacation. This wasn't the type of place someone pulled out words like that and used them in daily conversation.

"It just might at that."

Chapter Five

TREVOR SAT on the back deck of the resort, next to the pool, listening to the strains of music coming from the concert stage on the other side of the complex. He didn't want company, but just to sit and enjoy the balmy evening and scent of briny air coming off the ocean underscored by the chlorine in the pool.

It had been a pretty damn good day all the way around. Surfer Boy had been fun and interesting. The most important thing, he—Trevor—had baby-stepped out of his comfort zone and into the land of the living. And he liked it.

The zing of excitement soared through his blood like an emotional contact high. Man, it had been a long time since he'd felt this way. He just wanted to hang on to it for as long as possible and for the night to never end.

God, it felt weird to actually enjoy himself doing anything other than work. His life had become one long boardroom meeting without a break.

He shook that thought from his head.

There was safety and structure in work. It was out there in the world, where events were free flowing and chaotic, that life went to shit.

A hole opened right under his heart. The same pit that threatened to swallow him every time he thought of the past.

He picked up his drink and took a sip to ease the lump in his throat. It was a long time ago and he needed to forget, but he couldn't. That day haunted him like the specter of a fresh ghost.

The events of that evening eight years ago had impacted his life and changed it so significantly he no longer recognized the man he was back then—nor did he want to. The fault was his, and he'd never forgive himself for it.

Nor should he.

The night air had lost its magic. Any good feelings he'd had about the day with Surfer Boy were drowned by guilt.

Why should he be allowed to enjoy himself when….

He cut the thought off and walked into the lobby and to the elevators. What was there left to do but take a shower and hit the sheets? Plus he had an early appointment with the divemaster in the morning.

Maybe he should cancel.

No!

If he cancelled, he'd sit around the hotel and wonder what he was going to do to fill the hours and drive away the despairing thoughts. Guilt, shame, and unworthiness would snowball until he was drawn up into a fetal position and immobile.

This was the reason staying busy was always the best policy. Keeping his mind active and creative juices flowing was the only cure when the past reared up and tried to bite him on the ass.

What he needed tonight was a big dose of comfort in a pair of strong arms. He thought of Surfer Boy and shame heated his face. Yes, he wanted *those* arms and *those* lips to drive it all away, but he also wanted to remember the name he'd been given in that poolside bar with the loud music.

There was something inherently wrong with meeting someone and letting them get close without having the slightest clue on the name. And what if things got hot and heavy and he slipped and called him Surfer Boy—especially when he'd never mentioned surfing.

Trevor stopped in his tracks.

But he had mentioned diving.

And Trevor had seen him hanging around the boats moored near the pier where the dive shack was located.

Could it be possible?

Trevor really wanted to ask someone what Clive the Divemaster looked like—get a description. Did he happen to own a foulmouthed parrot?

He let out an audible groan and swiped a hand down his face. Without even having lived through it yet, he knew come morning he'd find Surfer Boy had morphed into Clive the Diver. Seriously, he didn't even have to think hard on it. In his heart he knew the truth.

Of course Surfer Boy was a master of something besides loincloth wrestling. He was a golden god of vacations everywhere. The kind of man both sexes looked to and envied. The kind of man who floated through life without direction, goals, or regrets.

The kind of man Trevor had never understood.

He put the keycard in the door and waited for the little light to turn green. The lock disengaged with a buzz. He pushed the door open and stepped into the cool air of his suite.

Instead of heading for the shower, he flopped down on the bed and covered his face with his arms. Jason would have told him to stop being so fucking dramatic and grow a pair.

And he'd be right.

Jason had always been the stabilizing force in his life—well, until *that* day. Then he'd had to learn to rely on nothing but himself and his ever-tightening grip on control. Nothing was ever for certain—the future especially—and happily-ever-afters were a fairytale.

Not that Surfer Boy represented any sort of a happily-ever-after, or even a happy-in-the-meantime. However, he was the kind of guy who made someone believe in a happy-in-the-moment.

Trevor dangled his feet over the side of the bed and kicked off his shoes. They hit the carpet with a dull thud. He rolled over onto his side and closed his eyes, imagining Jason still there on the bed beside him.

Aw hell. It was going to happen again. He was going to go spiraling down into a mood he wouldn't crawl out of anytime soon.

He hugged a pillow to his chest and closed his eyes against the wave of fresh pain that seemed to hit him out of some dark corner, an unsuspecting squirrel crossing a dark street with a car bearing down. There was no hope for the squirrel and no hope for him. He'd just have to ride out the emotion and wish for the best.

Strains of an old country tune came pouring from his phone.

He sat up as if he'd been electrocuted by the bed linens. The screen blinked the name Thompson along with the avatar of a horse's ass.

He pulled the phone from his pocket and swiped a finger across the screen. "Donohue."

Music blared from the background. It sounded like a party was going on and Thompson none the wiser.

Did the jerk just butt dial him, or was there a crisis at Global?

Trevor raised his voice a bit. "Hello."

When he still had no response, Trevor disconnected the line. Thompson had probably sat on his phone again. Last month he'd done that and phoned one of their affiliates in Holland. It had happened during a meeting where Thompson had been trashing one of their products because it had not as yet been approved by the FDA, and it didn't look as if it was going to happen in the near future. After the incident, it had fallen on Trevor's shoulders to call up the vendor and explain the situation, though he'd really wanted to hang Thompson out to dry.

Geoff had put his foot down. Instead of firing Thompson, Trevor had been forced to move him to a different project. Sometimes he wondered if Thompson was sucking Geoff's dick.

He set his phone on the bedside table and dared it to ring again.

Funny how for the better part of a week he'd wanted nothing more than to hear from someone at Global. When he did, it was the person he wanted to hear from the least. Even if it wasn't a real call.

Trevor got off the bed and grabbed his tablet. Quickly he pulled up Global's website and went to the blog. Any new announcement would be made there after it had been dispersed through the interoffice e-mail.

Nothing fresh appeared on the blog but new product information and a testimonial written by a customer that had run in a paper local to the corporate offices. Geoff thought it would be good PR to place it on the blog. Snippets of it were on the website as well.

He opened his e-mail and found a message from Trisha Vanderveer, the assistant VP who worked under him. With a pounding heart, he opened the e-mail and skimmed the page. It wasn't anything to fear.

"Wish I was there and you were here. I could use a long vacation."

He smiled at the typical Trisha line and even heard her dry delivery as he read it. She didn't mention anything other than she missed him around the office.

He typed an appropriate response and offered to change places with her. His phone buzzed with a text.

"Hey! I thought you'd have hooked up with a hot Latin lover by now."

Trevor huffed and smiled at the unlikely scenario. Trisha knew he didn't date often and tended to enjoy relationships that looked as if they were going somewhere other than straight to bed.

He typed, *"He's not Latin and he's not my lover—yet."*

What came back was a series of emoticons more suitable for a teenage girl's texted response than a woman with an MBA. Trevor laughed. He'd always liked Trisha, and they worked well together. She tended to be a little stricter on their team than Trevor, but she got results and respect and that was all that mattered. If Geoff were to promote someone, Trevor could only hope it was Trisha. She deserved it like no one else at Global.

He wrote back and forth to her for a few more minutes before she said she had to go put the kids to bed.

"If Geoff asks, I never texted, e-mailed, or spoke to you while you were gone. He'd have my head."

Trevor doubted that, but he gave her the reassurances she'd asked for. At least she wanted to keep in touch with him enough to defy Geoff's mandate. Oh, he could just imagine some of the rumors Thompson started when that order came down the pipeline.

The rest of the company probably didn't contact him because they thought he'd been fired. As if.

Trevor had never been fired. He'd left the medical profession of his own accord. He'd not been asked to leave or even summarily disciplined. If anything, his colleagues had begged him to stay, but offered their support when he'd decided to hang up his stethoscope for good.

Overall it had been a good choice for him. Saved his life no matter how ironic that seemed. However, he had kept his medical license in good standing even though he no longer practiced bedside care.

He changed into his pajama bottoms and pulled the covers back. He set the alarm and turned off the lamp.

Moonlight filtered in through the window, creating long shadows across the bedroom. The problem with vacationing in paradise was the one person he'd want to share it with was gone. Enjoying himself in the sun, drinking tropical drinks, and munching authentic local cuisine felt a betrayal.

He closed his eyes and tried to bring up Jason's face in his memory, but every time it blurred a little more around the edges. Eight years wasn't too long to forget the love of a lifetime. It was a drop in the bucket really. Would Jason have forgotten *his* face so easily?

Trevor rolled to his side and drew his knees up toward his chest. The thoughts alone were enough to cripple, to paralyze. Yet he knew deep down he had to move past this. He had no other choice now that he was on the island and had no work to sustain him or keep his mind occupied. God in heaven, he didn't even have any friends down here to call on. No one to pick him up out of this funk, except a man who ran hot and cold with regular frequency.

There had to be a story there. People just didn't become expats for no reason. He doubted if Surfer Boy's story was anywhere near as horrific and emotional as Trevor's. Surfer Boy just didn't seem to have that kind of passion in him. Not that he wasn't passionate. Sexually speaking, he was hotter than the mouth of a live volcano. But emotionally, he was a cold sesame noodle.

Trevor's breath caught. He had to admit, Surfer Boy had looked mighty damn hot when he'd retained his title of champion. Not to mention when he'd punched the fucker who shoved him like a schoolyard bully.

The exchange of words following the incident had been too rapid for Trevor to pick up on exactly what had happened to provoke the challenger. Surfer Boy blew off the incident, but he hadn't seen the man's face. Trevor had. That was not a face of momentary anger. It was a long-held grudge that had finally reached critical mass. It made Trevor very uncomfortable.

He rolled over again and beat at the pillow to make it more comfortable. Sleep was going to be a hard-fought battle. The more he thought about it, the more awake he became. He'd entered into the horrible mind-racing-versus-sleep-needing vortex that, once breached, was impossible to climb out of again.

Hell in a handcart, he hadn't experienced this level of wakefulness at night in years. Granted, most of the time he fell into bed too exhausted from the day to move a muscle, but he liked it that way. It worked for him.

Not tonight. That shower was sounding better by the minute. He slid out of bed again and headed for the bathroom, stripping his pajama pants down his legs as he went.

Cool tile felt good on his feet. He wiggled his toes as he stood at the shower stall and adjusted the water. A nice warm spray ran up his arm. Not too hot in the tropical heat and not so cold that he froze his balls off.

With the water temperature perfect, he stepped inside and attempted to wash away the stress and memories. He bowed his head forward, letting the jets hit the back of his neck in a pulsing massage.

God, that felt good. Maybe he'd find the resort spa at some point and book a real massage to help relieve some of the tension. It certainly couldn't hurt.

He and Jason used to go to a spa in the Village when they were both students at NYU. The woman who owned the place was a Swede who looked like she should have been an Olympic powerlifter, but damn did she give the best massages. He and Jason would practically roll home like two pats of melted butter, and were worthless for the rest of the day.

Sweet memories like those hurt the worst.

He picked up the soap and worked up lather. When the sweet ones hit, it was best to just push forward and keep moving, pretend they never happened.

But they had.

Every last one of them had been the cornerstone of the man he'd become.

He'd loved Jason with everything inside him. They had talked about the future and forever. They'd planned to grow old together.

Sorrow lodged in his belly.

Jason would have wanted him to live and move on, but for some reason he stayed stuck in time, unable to find the one miracle to fill the empty places.

A vision hot as the Santa Juanita sun filled his head and shook his body. Surfer Boy oil-slicked and wearing nothing but a loincloth and a knowing smile.

A moan fell from Trevor's lips. Now, that man was as close to a miracle as anything in this world. Instant arousal roared through his body, hardening his cock.

Indulgence in a little late-night fantasy wasn't going to hurt anyone, and it sure as hell guaranteed he'd sleep like a baby.

He wrapped a soapy hand around his cock and gave in to the feel of long slow strokes. It had felt so good when Surfer Boy had teased and cupped him with those large thick fingers. Trevor's heart had almost stopped at the pure bliss of the act. But then he'd felt unworthy of such happiness, of such betrayal—even if it was only to a memory.

An image of Jason superimposed itself over the lines of Surfer Boy's face. They were not that different in coloring. But where Jason had been lanky with the vestiges of youth, Surfer Boy was honed, hard, and all man.

Trevor tightened his fist, pumping his hips forward, imagining slamming his cock into Surfer Boy's waiting mouth. No way was he going to last with thoughts like that pouring into his head. Surfer Boy's sinner's eyes looking up at him and that sexy quirk in the corner of his mouth.

He leaned his forehead against the shower wall and closed his eyes. His balls tensed and the delicious sensation of orgasm screamed through his cock. He gave in to the moment and let the rush come. His legs shook, and he squatted on the floor before he fell and broke his head open on the tile.

After a few moments, he finished bathing and turned off the water. He dried off, but didn't bother to put his pajamas back on. It seemed sleep had come at last.

CLIVE GLANCED at his watch and up to the resort proper. No one was on the docks or even heading toward the pier. He turned back and frowned at Juan Pablo.

"Did you confirm with him?"

"I left a message on his room phone." Juan Pablo shrugged as if it meant nothing. However, they both knew Clive hated when tourists believed his time wasn't valuable. It was. Though he might dress like a beach bum and live in a casual atmosphere, for him time was money.

Having a private lesson booked meant he had to wait and take others out for dives later in the day. Not that it was all that early, but he could have taken a group out already and been back to base.

Vibrations on the wooden dock under his feet made him look up as Hookup came down the pier toward him. Well at least there was something to smile about, though he looked kind of rough around the edges this morning. Dark glasses hid the deep brown eyes from sight.

Clive waited until Hookup was in front of him and said, "You drink too much local tequila last night?"

"No. Just had a hell of a time sleeping. Kept waking up from bad dreams." Hookup rubbed his belly and made a face.

"You aren't coming down with something, are you?"

Hookup shook his head. "I can keep it together."

"Look, I'm going to be busy for a while. I have a refresher to do on a tourist, and I don't know how much I'll need to go over. If he ever shows." Clive looked down at the name on the clipboard and then to the people moving along the docks to get on boats.

Hookup's mouth twisted into a semblance of a grin. "I think you're waiting on me."

Clive read the name on the sheet. "Donohue?"

"That's me." Hookup—Trevor Donohue—looked over the tops of his expensive sunglasses. "You didn't remember my name."

The accusation shot color and heat to Clive's cheeks. It had been many years since he'd been so caught off guard or embarrassed. "I'm so busted."

Trevor waved his hand in a dismissing manner. "No sweat, man. I only connected the dots on your name late last night."

Clive gave a laugh caught somewhere between incredulousness and surprise. "That what gave you nightmares? That I was going to be your dive instructor?"

"No. Old problems that never seem to go away."

Trevor didn't say anything more, so Clive let it drop. The guy looked so damn unhappy, Clive was half-afraid to take him into the water for fear he'd drown himself.

"All right. I guess let's go over to the pool and get started."

"The pool?" Trevor made a face. "We're not going into the water down here?"

Clive shook his head. He picked up a couple of bags of equipment and handed one to Trevor. "No. I want to see you swim first. I can see better in a pool than I can in the ocean. I don't pass anyone on if they aren't strong swimmers. That's my bottom-line policy."

"All right. Let's go." Trevor took the bag and fell into line beside Clive.

As they walked up to the resort complex proper, Clive glanced over a few times, but Trevor was a silent partner.

"If you don't want to do this, we don't have to. I'll refund a percentage of your money."

Trevor gave a bark of sound. "A percentage?"

"I have to be paid for my time. I could have taken a party out to dive the galleon this morning." Clive stopped and held the clipboard in front of him. "This is my job, and I take it very seriously. Just because I work out of a kiosk doesn't mean it's not a business."

Trevor put his hand up. "I didn't mean to imply it isn't."

Clive glanced down the beach before settling his gaze once again on Trevor's handsome face. "I'm serious, though. You can reschedule if you want."

Trevor shook his head. "No, man. It's good. We'll do this now. And I'm sorry I was late getting down here. I probably could use a swim right about now to lose some of this tension."

There was a pool connected to the resort gym that was used only for those who wanted to do laps without having to swim around vacationers playing in their lane. Clive walked Trevor to the gym and stepped inside. There were only a few people in there at the moment. One was a grandmotherly type who swam at a slow and steady pace, but had good form. The other was the silver fox he'd taken out on the boat a few days before.

He nodded hello to the silver fox and waited for Trevor to strip off his clothes. Trevor kicked off his shoes and got out of his shirt and shorts. Clive tried not to stare at the body before him, but it was damn hard. The guy was simply built like a freaking statue of the male ideal.

Trevor stepped to the end of the pool and dove in. He moved under the water sleek as a shark to about midpool, where he resurfaced and started swimming in very strong strokes. Oh yeah, this guy had done this a time or two. Clive bet he'd spent a few years on swim teams.

Trevor went about six laps before Clive walked to the end of the pool and hunched down on the side.

Trevor came up and hung onto the side. "Good enough?"

"Like a pro." Clive held up his watch. "I want to see how long you can hold your breath."

Trevor ran a hand down his wet face. The man had no idea how good he looked wet and slick.

"Shouldn't you have done that before I swam those laps?"

"Nope. I want to see how long you can hold your breath once you've expended energy, not after you've rested. When you're out there in the ocean underwater, swimming around, and your regulator breaks, and your dive partner's malfunctions, you're not going to have the advantage of being perfectly rested. Besides, you've already taken big lungfuls of air while you've been swimming. All those tiny air sacs in there have expanded. You'll be in a better position to take a deeper breath now." Clive looked at his watch. "Go."

Trevor took a deep breath and submerged to the bottom.

Small bubbles rose to the surface. He was down there for a little over a minute—more than a respectable time for someone who hadn't dived for eight years.

Clive reached down and gave Trevor a hand out of the pool.

"Damn. I didn't bring a towel down." Trevor picked up his shirt and starting drying off with it.

"Hold on. There are some over at the reception desk." Clive jogged over and picked one up from the girl manning the pool counter. Why he didn't think to pick one up on their way in, he had no idea. Trevor kind of muddled his mind half the time. And damn, he'd totally walked into that whole not knowing his name thing earlier. Fucking embarrassing.

Heat filled his cheeks with remembered humiliation. It was one thing to not remember a guy's name. Quite another to be caught at it.

He handed the towel to Trevor.

Trevor? That name just didn't fit him. Trevor was the name of a stuffy Brit with a proper accent. Not a guy from Jersey with a hint of Bergen County in his voice. Oh, yes. Clive knew an accent from home when he heard it. There was no mistaking it.

Trevor dried off and whisked the towel through his hair. It looked even better mussed, if that was possible. The dude was too delicious for his own good. Even more so on closer acquaintance.

"What now?"

"Now we get to go over the equipment piece by piece. I want to see how much you remember. Then after we get all settled, we're going to run through a pool dive. I need to evaluate several areas, how much weight you'll need, buoyancy, and how well you control all the factors involved."

Trevor gave a half grin. "Wow. That brings back memories."

"Good ones, I hope." Clive opened one of the bags and started pulling out the equipment they'd need, then lined it up along the edge of the pool. "First I want to see if you can name everything here and what it's used for."

"Oh man." Trevor ran a hand through his hair. "I didn't even think that there'd be a quiz involved. I just thought you'd make me dive and see if I did it right."

"Not me. Not when your safety is on the line. I never second-guess that. It makes for bad policy."

Clive watched Trevor closely as he glanced at the equipment array and started with the most obvious.

"Tanks. They hold the air the diver breathes during the dive. Regulator. Attaches to the tank and allows the diver to breathe."

"Is that a first stage or second stage regulator?"

Trevor picked up the device and smiled. "That's a trick question, right?"

"No. Not at all. I want to know that you know which is which." Clive folded his arms in front of him and waited.

"First. Second." Trevor indicated the pieces correctly.

"What do you do with the first stage regulator?"

"Attach it to the tank."

When Trevor didn't do it, Clive gave him a raised brow. "Well, go ahead and do it."

Trevor preformed the task in a seamless manner.

They went through the rest of the gear in a relatively short time. Some of the newer equipment, like the dive computer, Trevor had never used, but that wasn't anything that would make Clive deny Trevor the right to dive on the island, especially with him as divemaster.

"All right." Clive looked down at his watch. "Let's put it all together and do a pool dive so I can check you off."

So far, for not having done a dive in eight years, Trevor had managed to make few mistakes and seemed more than competent with the equipment.

The pool dive went much the same way. They only spent about twenty minutes in the pool where Clive tested Trevor on hand signals, buoyancy, and a few other concepts.

They climbed back out of the pool and dried off.

"What do we do now?" Trevor ruffled his hair with the towel. It stood up in sexy messiness.

"Now we grab something to eat."

Trevor glanced up with a raised brow. "Really?"

Clive considered it for a moment. What he really wanted to do was take Trevor to the bungalow and spend the rest of the day with him. There was a dive scheduled for the next day. A big one with a group of six who wanted to go out to the galleon.

"Yes, really. I'm hungry. Let's take a walk, and I'll show you around the area a bit. We'll grab some lunch, and you can come dive the galleon with me and a group I'm taking out tomorrow. How does that sound?"

A smile curled the corner of Trevor's mouth. Clive had the overwhelming urge to lean over and kiss him there. He refrained.

"Sounds like a plan." Trevor stepped into his shorts, then pulled his shirt on, leaving it unbuttoned. "Afterward I might go for a walk along the beach. I haven't really done much exploring here the past few days. Feeling like I'm at loose ends has kind of thrown me off a bit."

"I hear you." They started walking out of the pool area and used the door that led outside. "When I left the corporate world back home, it took me a few weeks to get used to having a less-structured life, but it happens."

Trevor stopped and touched Clive's arm. "Wait. You worked in the corporate world? You? Mr. Divemaster?"

"What? Did you think I've done this all my life?" Clive gave Trevor a knowing smile, trying not to let the hand on his arm distract him too much or enjoy the weight of Trevor's fingers on his skin. "I did the whole college, get-a-good-job thing. My parents wouldn't have had it any other way." The thought of which made acid bathe the back of his throat. "To say they were pissed when I chucked it all and moved an entire continent away is understating the drama of the moment."

They started down the steps as if by mutual agreement to begin moving again. "Hard to believe you actually admitted that."

It was hard for Clive to believe as well. He never shared anything even close to personal with men he'd hooked up with while they were vacationers. There seemed little point. But for some reason, Trevor, from the very first meeting, was different. At the risk of going all clichéd and sappy about the situation, Trevor had a kindred spirit to him that Clive had a hard time denying.

Clive gave a shrug. "Don't tell anyone I did. You'll ruin my reputation as mysterious."

This time Trevor gave a deep laugh that rumbled through Clive's insides, upsetting his equilibrium. He gripped the handrail as he continued down the stairs, afraid if he didn't, he'd fall off the world.

Yes. This was big. Huge. His feelings were traveling at Mach 2 away from casual and into the realm of places he didn't wish to go, and he could do nothing about it but sit back and wait for the train wreck to happen.

They returned to the kiosk so Clive could pick up any messages from Juan Pablo before heading back home.

Juan Pablo scratched his cheek, then wiped a hand around his mouth as if reluctant to say anything.

"What is it?" Clive found the behavior unusual. Something was up.

"Man came here asking if you were around. When I said I'd give you a message when you came back, he didn't want to leave that or a name. He left, cutting through the track to the village."

It was odd but nothing to worry over. "He didn't look familiar?"

"No. That's what I found strange. He wasn't one of the locals, and he doesn't work at the resort."

"Maybe he's from the resort on the other side of the island." Clive brushed off the incident. If it was about business, the guy would come back. If not, no sweat.

He handed the tanks to Juan Pablo to store, then turned to Trevor. "Let's go up to my bungalow for some lunch. I have to check on Rodger anyhow."

"I don't want to put you out."

Clive gave Trevor what he hoped was a gentle smile. "You won't be. It's lunch, not a seven-course banquet."

Trevor's cheeks turned pink. "All right. I accept."

Clive showed him the route over the jetties. It was a beautiful view of the water and shoreline for as far as the eye could see. The coast stretched around in sugar-white sands that met the cool blue-green of the water.

Clive pointed past the bluff and out to the horizon. "If you go straight that way and out a few miles, you come to the site of the galleon."

"So close to shore when they wrecked." Trevor shaded his eyes as if looking into the past.

"And a tragic tale, too, though how much of it was real and how much is local mythos is debatable." Clive started walking again, picking his way over the rocks to the bluff.

"So what's the story?" Trevor followed him. They stood on the overlook, casting their gazes into the distance.

"It goes that a Spanish explorer by the name of Rodrigo Suarez y Rioz sailed across the ocean in search of the woman he loved, who had been captured and taken abroad by a rival for her affection, one Gutierrez deChamplian.

"He'd crossed back and forth from Central America to South and back again. Finally, he heard news of her on the mainland. A woman fitting her description had been seen in town, face covered in a veil, with the sheen of tears shining behind the gossamer fabric.

"Rodrigo set sail for the island, heedless of the weather and warnings in the sky. The ship went down in a hurricane off the coast, only miles from their destination.

"Miraculously, Rodrigo survived and washed ashore. He was taken in and cared for by nuns in the Catholic abbey." Clive pointed off to the west. "You can still see the ruins of the abbey." He started walking again. "Juanita, the woman in question, had heard her lover was coming for her and then about the shipwreck. Not realizing he'd survived, she threw herself from the rocks and killed herself. When he woke and realized she'd killed herself believing him dead, he found her grave and killed himself on top of it. They were together at last, in death."

Clive turned to Trevor and was startled to see he had removed his sunglasses and was wiping at his eyes. Clive didn't say anything, but let him alone in his grief.

Trevor fell into line behind Clive. After a long silence, broken only by the sounds of the surf crashing against the shoreline and the squawk of seabirds, Trevor said, "That's very Romeo and Juliet."

"Agreed. I think maybe that's where the locals took a lot of the legend from, but I have no way to prove it. Historians on the mainland haven't confirmed or denied the legend, and I don't think they really want to. It's good for the tourist trade and local economy, so they tend to take a more pragmatic approach." Clive stood at the head of a well-worn path. "It's this way, just a little bit ahead."

"So the island is named after this Juanita?"

"Supposedly. It's the Santa part that's always made me rather suspicious. San Juan, all right, I get that named after Saint John. But to take the female aspect of the name or to suggest that the Juanita who is tied to the story of the island was a saint is stretching it a bit." Clive turned to walk backward up the slight incline as he talked to Trevor. "Not that she did anything wrong, or even deserved to be carted off by some guy she didn't love to parts unknown, but there is nothing in the record to suggest she did anything worthy of sainthood."

"So your conclusion is the name of the island and the story are completely separate incidents." Trevor slid his hands into his pockets and started to climb. Strong calf muscles bulged at the effort, drawing Clive's gaze downward.

"Yes. Exactly." Clive swiped his hand in the air in a sign of victory. Someone had finally gotten his point and didn't seem offended by the difference of opinion. Locals loved their legend even if it had only the barest origins in fact. "I think it's more likely named after Saint John the way other towns with the same name have done. Considering the abbey that once stood there was dedicated to Saint John, I think I have a pretty good historical leg to stand on."

Trevor gave him a smirk. "And the historians on the mainland look the other way?"

"Like I said, it all comes down to tourists and revenue."

"But being right is important to you?"

Clive thought about it for a moment. "Not especially. I just like it when people agree with me."

Trevor smiled and shook his head. "You are something and a half, man."

The offhanded compliment made Clive burn all the way through his skin. It felt good to just be enjoyed as a person and not for his sexual prowess.

He swallowed down the panic raised by getting into that danger zone. Damn but Trevor played hell with his peace of mind.

They came up over the hill. His house stood in the shade of a few trees but opened up to the wide expanse of the bluff.

"Well, this is it."

Clive unlocked the sliders and opened the back door, then stepped aside to allow Trevor to walk through first.

"Intruder alert! Intruder alert!"

"No Rodg, it's only me and Trevor."

"Hot damn."

Clive chuckled and walked to the perch. "How's my favorite little guy?"

"Looking for love in all the wrong places," the bird sang and danced across the wooden bar.

"You haven't been looking for anything today." Clive picked him up and set the bird on his shoulder.

"Want the hottie. Want the hottie."

Clive smiled as Trevor's face burned. "I think he means you."

"I'll hold him while you do whatever it is you were going to do." Trevor came closer and stood still as Clive transferred Rodger over. "Hey there."

Clive grabbed a handful of sunflower seeds and laid them in Trevor's hand. "Here, give him a few of these. One at a time, please."

"Peel me a grape, big boy." The bird really needed to get a handle on his vocabulary.

Trevor handed a seed up, which Rodger took very delicately with a foot. "At least you aren't spewing profanities today."

Rodger munched happily on his seed and didn't bother to answer.

Clive went into the kitchen and started pulling things out of the fridge and cabinets. "How does pasta carbonara sound?"

"Like it's loaded with fat and calories. Right up my alley."

Clive raised a brow. "You're kidding, right? You don't look like you ingest anything that isn't high protein and low glycemic index."

Trevor's face pinked up again. "I've been known to indulge."

Christ, he hadn't meant anything sexual by that, but he felt a little hot himself with the thought of getting protein in a most pleasant way. Clive chuckled to cover his own embarrassment.

He cleared his throat, then said, "I suppose having been trained in medicine you try to eat healthy."

Trevor made a face as if he never thought about it much. "My parents were sticklers for proper diet, so it was just something I grew up doing—habit. I don't even really think about it now. It's just second nature."

Clive set a pan on the stove and turned on the heat. He added some fresh butter and let that melt for a bit while he prepped the garlic and set water on to boil. Cooking was one of the few domestic chores he did that actually relaxed him. He enjoyed watching raw ingredients come together to make a cohesive whole.

And at the moment, he really could use a way to relax. If he didn't keep focused and concentrate, he was going to slam his body into Trevor's and start getting down and dirty with the poor, unsuspecting dude.

"You have quite the setup here." Trevor's voice piercing through the sound of chopping startled Clive. Not because he'd forgotten he was there—damn, who could—but because Trevor seemed content to sit there and stroke Rodger.

Clive glanced over his shoulder. "I gutted the place and rebuilt it to my specifications. It was a bitch getting some of the building materials from the mainland, but I managed." It had taken bribes, finesse, and free dive lessons in order to get all the things he'd required.

The only concession he'd not been willing to make was skipping the full-size fridge. He hated those useless, fucking mini ones that were so popular in homes all over the island. The transportation of a larger one from the States had been very costly but well worth it.

"It's… cozy." Trevor stood and started for the main living space. "Mind if I take an unguided tour?"

"No. Go for it. Knock yourself out."

Clive breathed a sigh of relief as Trevor left the room. What had he been thinking bringing the man here? Suddenly it didn't seem such a good idea, since he'd felt nothing but tense and tingly since they'd stepped inside the bungalow.

This was so not like him.

It was like one of those damn 1950s horror movies where an alien pod from another planet came down and inhabited the body of an unsuspecting main character. He was being controlled by an alien pod—that had to be the answer.

He stirred in the bacon and chopped onions. Flavorful steam billowed up to his nose. The water began to boil, and he stuck in the fresh pasta he'd frozen a few weeks before.

No sounds came from the rest of the house. Clive listened intently, but there was nothing. Not even the continuous crack of sunflower seed shells.

Damn, he was in a critical phase of the lunch preparation. There wasn't time to go and find out where Trevor had taken the damn bird. Clive tried to put it out of his mind. When lunch was ready, he'd call out for Trevor, and if he didn't respond, then he'd go looking for him. If he didn't show, then Clive would eat alone—then find Trevor and break his leg for a bird thief.

Chapter Six

TREVOR LOOKED out over the bluff and the majestic expanse of the ocean. The mainland wasn't even a line on the horizon. From this vantage point, the island looked isolated and removed from civilization. The resort wasn't even visible from this particular location. No wonder Clive chose to call it home. It was simply breathtaking.

Be it mythos or pseudo-history, Trevor didn't care one way or the other, the story of Rodrigo and Juanita had broken open a wound a mile wide in him. Thankfully Clive hadn't seen the tears Trevor had tried so hard to hide. Hearing that tragic love story on the heels of a night spent thinking and dreaming about Jason had pushed him a bit close to the edge.

Christ, he'd woken to the alarm thinking it was the wail of sirens from the night Jason died. It had taken a moment to realize where he was and that the warm wash on his skin was sweat and not blood. It had taken another thirty minutes and a second shower to stop his hands from shaking.

"It's ready!" Clive called from the house.

"Come and get it!" Rodger squawked in the best aviary impersonation of Granny Clampett Trevor had ever heard.

Trevor reached up and petted the parrot as he turned back to the bungalow. "You are something else, my friend."

"Hot damn! Getting laid."

Trevor couldn't help but laugh. "No. I don't think so."

Clive had set the patio table with dishes and a covered serving bowl. "What would you like to drink?"

"Anything but tap water." Trevor glanced down at the settings. "You didn't have to go to so much trouble."

Clive stalled at the sliding doors. "What trouble? It was a quick meal, and the view out here is better."

Trevor couldn't argue there. It was a spectacular view. And to imagine the guy lived like this year 'round. It amazed and ashamed Trevor just thinking about all the horrible winter commutes on Jersey roads. To think Clive only had to roll out of bed and walk down to the resort to be at work?

All right, so maybe Trevor wouldn't know what to do with all the free time. And maybe it would drive him crazy not having some kind of structure to his life, but there could be a lot said for living in paradise. At least this corner of it.

Clive came back outside carrying two glasses of what looked like a fruity concoction. "You might enjoy this. It's a popular local drink. Five kinds of citrus juice and honey. Nothing in it that's bad for you."

Trevor took the offered glass and held it to his nose and sniffed. It smelled good. Refreshing and clean. He took a tentative sip. "That is good, but how is it going to taste with your lunch?"

"It will cleanse the palate with each sip. You'll see." Clive waved Trevor to a chair. "Sit down and dig in."

Trevor did as told. At the first bite, his eyes rolled back in his head. "All right, this is amazing."

"It's all the fresh ingredients. Nothing here is processed. It makes a difference."

"I'll say." Actually the food at Clive's was better than what the master chefs made at the resort. "If that diving gig ever dries up, you have a second career right here."

Clive smiled as he chewed. "No. I like cooking for myself and a few select people. If I had to do it for a couple hundred to thousand people a day, I'd probably want to cut my wrist with a carving knife."

"That bad, huh?"

"Yes. I see what the chefs at the resort get put through on a daily basis, and I want no part of it."

"Where did you get your philosophy?" When Clive looked as if he was offended, Trevor held up a hand. "No. I'm serious. You live on this beautiful spot, work in a job you love, which probably doesn't seem like a job at all, and you're happy. What's your secret?"

Clive leaned back in his chair. "I paid my dues as a younger man and decided I didn't want to live under someone else's cloud of bullshit the rest of my life. Pretty straightforward."

Yes, it was, and it was freaking brilliant. It was one of those things that people on self-help DVDs told people to do, but meeting someone in the flesh who had actually had the balls to go and do it and make it happen was rather awe inspiring.

In that moment of self-reflection, with the scent of the ocean on the air and gentle wind blowing across the bluff, Trevor realized for the first time in many years how truly unhappy he was with his life. The thought was sobering enough to make his stomach roil and pitch.

"Is something wrong?" Clive leaned forward and laid his hand on top of Trevor's. "You don't look so good."

Trevor shook his head, denying the need for concern. He turned his hand over and linked his fingers in Clive's. Hazel eyes rounded in shock for only a moment before Clive hooded his expression.

Trevor squeezed Clive's hand a bit tighter. "Thank you."

"For what?"

"Opening my eyes to some things I need to change."

MARLIE LEANED against Clive's chair. The pool bar was hopping, the music was loud, and people were in a festive mood.

Clive looked up from his beer as Marlie hip-checked him again. "What's going on?"

"I was going to ask you that. I heard you were seen all over the island the past few days with tall, dark, and yummy." Her eyes sparkled as if she'd been the one to introduce them or had a stake in the outcome.

Marlie was actually the closest thing he had to family after he'd given up his own and moved to the island. She was a younger sister and nagging mother all in one.

"Trevor. I don't know if I'd call the village and the bluff behind my house all over the island, but yeah, we've spent some time together." He took a sip of his beer, then set it back on the bar.

"And?"

"And what?" He tried not to smile, but the fact of the matter was Trevor made him feel better than he had in years, and it was scary as hell.

"Where is he?" She glanced around the pool area. "I don't see him."

Clive shook his head. "I don't know. We had lunch together at my place and then walked back down here. He went up to his room to take a nap, and I hung out at the kiosk."

Disappointment lowered her shoulders. "Oh. I thought you two would be getting hot and heavy by now."

"He's not the type to rush things." It seemed his policy to not kiss and tell had suddenly blown away on the trade winds. As if sensing his agitation, Rodger danced along his shoulder. Either that or the crazy bird really was dancing.

"The boy's hot!"

Marlie laughed and scratched Rodger behind the crown. "Is that right? How does he get along with Rodger?"

"He thinks the sun rises and sets by Trevor's command. Of course that means he's been extra generous with the profanities."

Marlie laughed. "That's awesome."

Carlos joined them, coming to stand on Clive's other side. He nodded in greeting to Clive and handed Rodger a peanut.

"Gracias, amigo."

Clive looked at Rodger. "When did you pick up Spanish?"

Rodger didn't answer. He put the peanut in his beak and cracked the shell.

"There was a guy out at the docks asking about you earlier."

"Juan Pablo told me." Clive lifted his beer to indicate to the bartender he wanted to order another one.

"No. This was about an hour ago. I guess he came back. Seemed really agitated you weren't there." Carlos looked off around the pool area. "I was there when he showed up before—same guy."

"Do you know him?"

"No. Suzanna said she thinks he's from the mainland. Runs one of the shuttle boats."

Clive thought about it for a moment. "If he does, he should give someone his name. I know all the guys from the shuttle boats."

"Just passing on the information."

"If you happen to see him again, do me a favor and take a picture with your phone. I want to see if I know the guy." Clive didn't like the idea someone was looking for him and not giving his name. It just seemed strange. If it was a tourist, they'd probably tell Juan Pablo or Carlos what they wanted. There were only so many services Clive provided. The list wasn't long by any stretch of the imagination. No sense in making a mystery out of nothing. Not to mention if it had something to do with his dive business, they'd say something or let Juan Pablo help them.

Carlos agreed, then ordered a drink.

Marlie leaned around Clive to get Carlos's attention. "You want to dance?"

Carlos smiled shyly into his drink. "Yes. Very much."

They took off for the dance floor, leaving Clive to nurse his beer in private. Or as private as he could get in a party. Living near the resort, he was rarely ever alone. Someone was always looking for him or needing to speak with him, which made the fact a lone man was hunting him down all the weirder.

He watched them as they took a place on the floor and began to dance. Carlos had it bad for Marlie, and as far as Clive knew, he'd never made his move—not formally. Clive was going to have to say something to the guy to let him know it was all right with him. After the Simon situation, most of the men interested in Marlie deferred to

Clive. Thing was, he thought Marlie and Carlos were perfect for each other, and the guy clearly adored her.

Clive's mind wandered back to his own problems. He'd considered more than once if it was Red who'd come to take another swing at him, but for what reason? Hell, he'd racked his brain the last few days trying to remember if he'd fucked the guy at some point.

Rodger started imitating the musical beat by making guttural sounds in the back of his throat near Clive's ear.

"Marlie should have asked you to dance."

"Hot damn!"

Clive gave a bark of sound and looked down into his beer bottle. "I think we should call it a night, buddy."

"Asshole."

Clive just shook his head. Rodger was a party animal, no doubt about it. "Come on. We have to get up early and go out on the boat."

"Diver down!"

He downed the rest of his beer and stood. The walk back to his place was long and deserted. Good, he really wasn't in the mood for company or to even talk to anyone. Trevor's compliments earlier in the day had forced him into a contemplative frame of mind he hadn't fallen into in a very long time.

He liked the fact he'd come to a point in his life where his future plans only included what he had scheduled until the next sunset. When he'd hooked up with Trevor that first night, he'd not meant for it to be a life-altering experience for the dude. He just wanted some hot sex and to leave it at that—not to feel responsible for changing the guy's life. Hell, Clive didn't need that kind of responsibility.

Didn't want it.

Sure, he thought Trevor needed to loosen up and enjoy life more, but the look on his face spoke of a deeper change than mere learning to relax.

Clive's own conversion had happened almost by chance. A horrible situation back in the States, a need to chuck his life and start over, and a vacation that never ended. It was the recipe for a perfect, stress-free life. Something had to come out of the pain and conflagration his life had disintegrated into. The fact he'd come out the other side whole and happy had been a miracle.

One he didn't like to dwell on often.

He was thankful for all he had now and would never wish to go back to his other life. Not for anything. Christ, it had been ten years since he'd heard anything from his friends back home.

Could he even call them friends now? Probably not. They were people who were part of his life for a short time, served their purpose, and moved on as he'd moved on.

He raked a hand through his hair and started up the hill to his bungalow. Visions of coming home to Trevor at the end of the day filled his head with things unlikely to ever happen.

Man was he ever getting ahead of himself.

Trevor was going to figure his life out, learn to slow down, and then go home. There was no use even pretending he was going to stay on the island. He really wasn't the type to give up all the luxuries of living so close to an urban center like New York.

Some men were made for clinging to the familiar, others for cutting off the things that didn't work and moving on. Trevor was the former and Clive the latter. He had to remember that or risk getting in over his head.

Thank God, they hadn't slept together.

Clive lifted his arms and put them behind his head as he walked. Rodger made a disgruntled noise and shifted on his shoulder.

"Stupid fucker!"

"Don't I know it."

"X marks the spot."

"What?" Clive turned to stare at Rodger in the dark. "I'm going to cut down on your movie privileges."

Rodger danced again. *"Let's do the rumba."*

"Silly bird."

He walked up the steps to his porch. A note hung on the front door. He tore it off and unlocked the door. Rodger took that opportunity to shit down his arm.

"Aw, Rodg. You couldn't have held it for a few more minutes?"

Clive set the note on the table by the door, then set Rodger on the back of the couch before heading to the bedroom. He stripped his shirt off as he went. At least it had happened when he was almost home and not in the middle of the bar. Though it wouldn't have been the first time Rodger bombed him in public.

"Rodger is a bad boy." The plaintive voice came from the back of the couch.

Clive rolled his eyes and stuck his head out of the bedroom door to look at the chastised parrot. "No. Rodger is a very good boy. Just give me a little warning next time, buddy. All right?"

Rodger started to dance and flap his wings. Instead of speaking he started making whistling noises.

Clive stripped down and jumped into the shower. Might as well get it over and done with while he was cleaning up. Then maybe he'd hit the sheets and get some rest, though truthfully he wasn't feeling all that tired. More keyed up and restless.

The blame lay squarely on Trevor's broad shoulders. If he'd only kept his mouth shut, Clive wouldn't have had a hard time thinking about any number of other things.

He pumped his hand into a fist a few times, remembering the feel of Trevor's hand as it rested on his.

He stepped under the spray and let the warm water sluice down his head, wetting his hair. Christ, he was already half-erect. The last thing he wanted was to stand in a shower and jack off. There was something a little sad and pathetic about that. Like he didn't have enough charm to get laid and had to turn to self-gratification to get off.

He closed his eyes and leaned his forehead against the shower wall. Bright brown eyes in a tanned olive-skinned face flashed in his mind. The vulnerable set of a wide, sexy mouth.

Clive moaned and turned the cold water on higher. His erection lengthened.

What had happened in Trevor's life to make him shed tears over a story that might not even be true or at the very least ripped off from

Shakespeare? Well, whatever it was, Clive was not going to get involved. It was none of his business.

That didn't stop the overwhelming urge to take Trevor into his arms and kiss all the pain away or the need to hold him tightly until dawn. It was a good thing Trevor had gone to his room early and avoided Clive. Temptation was too great, and Clive was fast losing the battle to maintain his cool.

Cold water caused pinpricks along his skin. His dick decided on a safe retreat. It was probably best that way. If he indulged in a little shower wanking, then he'd be more susceptible to wanting the real thing.

Tomorrow he'd try to think of a way to distance himself from Trevor. It was the only way to protect his heart.

He hurried through his bath and dried off, then fell into bed.

He didn't move until morning.

Chapter Seven

T REVOR STOOD on the dock waiting for the group to assemble. Clive had a clipboard and personally inspected every piece of equipment that went on the boat. Never let it be said that he took safety lightly.

Rodger sat on a perch, giving orders to anyone within earshot. The crew all ignored him, which made his language even more colorful than usual. Those waiting to go out on the boat laughed at the bird's antics.

Clive looked up and made a calling motion with his hand. "Trevor, climb onboard and calm Rodger down, will you?"

Trevor boarded down at the motor and made his way over to the agitated parrot. "What's the matter, little buddy?"

Rodger swiveled his brightly colored head. *"Hot stuff!"*

Trevor laughed and glanced up to find Clive looking at him with a heated expression in his gorgeous eyes before turning sharply away.

A band tightened around Trevor's chest. Air had a hard time passing through his lungs. He was going to fall for Clive, and there wasn't anything he could do about it. Problem was he didn't know if he should throw caution to the tropical wind and go for it, or start keeping a safe distance.

"What do you think, Rodger? Think I should make my move?"

"X marks the spot."

"In most cases, no, it doesn't. It's up to us to find the treasure on our own." Trevor let his gaze follow Clive as he finished preparations to take the group out.

His stomach rumbled with nerves. He'd done pretty well the day before. Most of the information had come back to him. He'd spent some time going over a book on diving tips before going to bed. He'd hate to get out there and do something stupid and put either himself or others in danger. Clive didn't seem the type to suffer fools lightly. As a matter of fact, when it came to his business, he was rather a hardass.

The rest of the group was allowed onboard. They all took seats. A man named Carlos operated the boat, taking them out to where the Spanish galleon lay at the bottom of the ocean.

Clive sat in the seat on the other side of Carlos but never once came close to Trevor. As a matter of fact, he'd made a point of ignoring him except for the earlier request to keep Rodger from offending the other tourists.

Feeling like a piece of rancid meat, Trevor sat there in silence and watched the horizon. What had he done? Yesterday they'd spent the day together. Today he was *persona non grata*.

Fine. He got it. He didn't need it pointed out to him. Clive was the type who wanted no strings and no commitments. That was all right by Trevor. He'd never asked for any, but he did think he deserved to at least be treated civilly. Not that Clive was hostile. No, it was more of a lumping him in with the other tourists.

And what was the big deal in that? Trevor *was* a tourist.

If Clive was worried Trevor had wanted something more by what he'd said yesterday at lunch, he was mistaken. It had been meant as an illumination on his own faults and failings, not as a means to cling onto someone who obviously was about as unavailable emotionally as a sunken Spanish galleon.

They dropped anchor and everyone began to don their dive suits. The divers were paired up. Trevor hung back, half decided against going in the water. He'd stay topside and keep Carlos and the other hand, Guillermo, company, maybe talk to Rodger.

Clive moved by him. "Aren't you coming?"

"Spanish galleons have kind of lost their luster. I'll stay up here."

"Suit yourself." Clive sat down and put on his fins. "Kind of seems a waste of renewing your certification."

"There'll be other times when I get back home." Though he doubted it. He'd fall back into the same pattern of work, sleep, work, sleep.

"Get moving, scalawag." Rodger shuffled, raising his feathers.

Clive raised a brow. "I think that was meant for you."

"At least he didn't call me a stupid fucker."

Trevor rose and moved to the end of the boat to allow Guillermo to help him into his equipment. His stomach lurched.

Please don't let me get the bends. The last thing he needed was to get shipped to the mainland for hyperbaric therapy—if they even had a chamber there.

His hand shook as he put the regulator in his mouth. It was all right. He'd done this before on several occasions with Jason. They'd go down to Cape May or head to Ocean City, Maryland to take the dive cruises. In no way was he considered a dive virgin.

Clive went into the water first, followed by the lead pair of dive buddies. As each group went overboard, Trevor's nerves ratcheted up another notch. There was no one to go over the side with him. He didn't have a buddy. Well, he could always go in and just keep the others within sight like he'd been taught.

The water looked pretty clear, even out this far from the coast. Guillermo gave Trevor the signal, and he went over the side, plunging into the warm, bath-like water.

Views, even this near the surface, were spectacular. The Spanish galleon sat like some great hulking whale carcass. Amazement that so much of the ship was still intact after so long sent a shiver of excitement through him. The only thing he thought of while gliding through the blue-green depths was getting closer to this marvel lost in time.

Clive swam up beside him and gave a thumbs-up. His eyes behind the mask danced as if seeing the wreck anew through Trevor's reaction.

They moved to the safety stop.

There were no words for the sad beauty and majesty of the grounded ship. It was plain to see why the ship had gone down. A reef was stretched across a plateau. Ribs of the great hull were cradled in the coral, and it was hard to tell where one began and the other ended. It had grown together, the coral twisting and turning skeletal hands toward the surface.

Colorful fish swam by in an ordered school. Some scattered when Trevor and Clive neared. An eel peeked out at them from beneath the side-lying bow.

Trevor kicked ahead. The masthead remained intact. The growth of sea life over the surface made detecting the carved image difficult. It might have been man, woman, or mythical creature. The fact it was still part of the wreck was impressive.

A look inside proved the treasures that had once been contained within were now gone, probably the center of some rich man's collection or in a museum on the mainland. Had it even been carrying gold or other riches? Maybe not, if the story was true and Rodrigo had gone searching for his lover. But then, expeditions were expensive undertakings; he'd had to have made the trip worth the expense and time.

Though some people did some pretty crazy stuff for love. Like turn their backs on their careers and forge new paths. Many times over the years Trevor had wanted to follow Jason into the grave, but he hadn't. He'd lived.

No. He'd existed.

As he swam around the old shipwreck, the evidence of someone following their heart to death, Trevor knew one sure thing—he never wanted to be *that* person again.

He'd loved Jason with an intensity and all-consuming obsession of youth, and he'd allowed that to shape his adulthood. It had been unhealthy and stifling.

Trevor came around the south end of the wreck. Shy fish hid in the hollows created by the twist of coral and wood. They moved back inside, away from the scary humans in scuba gear. In this area, the fish should have been used to seeing humans swim by. But maybe to a fish, they all looked like sharks. Even some of the bigger species moved out of the way. Crabs scuttled along the bottom of the wreck, trying to get out of the way of the beam of light Clive pointed in their direction.

They explored for a bit longer before Clive gave the signal to ascend. Slow and controlled. Trevor concentrated on his breathing and tried not to fall into rushing to the surface to compare notes with the other divers.

Clive stayed at the end of the boat in the water as all the divers came onboard. Trevor was the last one to board before Clive climbed up the ladder.

"All present and accounted for."

People started to clean their equipment and get it ready for storage. There was no such thing as being treated as a guest on one of Clive's dives. He made each diver care for their regulators and tanks, though he made a thorough inspection of them when they were placed in storage.

Trevor worked on his tanks and listened to the conversations around him, though he didn't participate.

"Hey, hot stuff!" The call came from midboat, where Rodger danced on his perch.

When Trevor finished cleaning the salt water from the equipment, he made his way back to the parrot and scratched him behind the crown. "Were you good while Clive was gone?"

"Jolly Rodger's a good boy."

"Yes, he is." Trevor had to admit he had a better rapport with the parrot than the man. "And the handsomest bird ever."

Rodger preened as if he understood the compliment. Trevor wouldn't be at all surprised. Clive came over and took a seat close to Rodger's perch. He glanced over at Trevor before looking away again.

All right, this was just getting weird and uncomfortable. There for a while in the water, it had seemed as if maybe the tension of the morning had all been in Trevor's mind. No such luck. It was back in full force.

Trevor gritted his teeth and choked down the disappointment and went to sit out in the sun to catch a few rays before they returned to dock. When they did return, he was going to go straight to the kiosk and find out how much this dive tour normally cost so he could reimburse Clive for the time.

Yes, he'd been invited, but he suddenly felt more like a leech than a guest. Never let it be said he didn't pay his way or that he took advantage of a situation. He so wasn't *that* guy.

They pulled into the marina, and Trevor waited for them to tie off the boat. He thanked Clive with a backward wave and made his way to the kiosk.

The same guy who had manned the booth the day he signed up for his lessons was there again, this time with a woman who looked like she'd stepped out of the Miss Brazil contest.

"Can I help you?" the woman asked as she leaned over the counter, showing more of her impressive bosom than should have been medically safe perched on the counter like that.

"Yes, I just returned from a dive tour and I need to pay."

The woman turned to look at her male counterpart and handed the transaction over to him as if she didn't want to touch it with a fishnet.

The man smiled and shook his head. "Do you want to see me unemployed?"

Trevor gave a huff that passed for a laugh. "No. Of course not. I'm just trying to do the honest thing here."

A frisson scudded over his skin. He knew without turning that Clive had walked up behind him.

"What are you doing?" Irritation painted Clive's voice.

"I'm trying to pay for the tour."

"Jesus Christ," Clive muttered. "Come on, let's take a walk."

"No. I'm good." Heat crept up Trevor's neck. He rubbed it as tension coiled. Judging from the look on Clive's face, he wasn't going to accept no—probably wasn't told no too often.

"Asshole!" Rodger danced.

Trevor turned his face to the wind and took a deep breath of the sea air. It was hard to keep a straight face after being insulted by a man's crusty parrot sidekick.

"Shh, Rodger." Clive hushed his bird and extended his arm, indicating the dock. "Please."

All right, that was the one word that ensured compliance. If Trevor didn't walk with Clive, he'd look like the asshole Rodger called him. He fell into step beside Clive. "You wanted to say something you didn't want your friends back there to hear?"

"Yes. I wanted to apologize."

Trevor felt his mouth quirk up at the corner. "And you couldn't be caught saying sorry to someone?"

"No. It's not that. It's just that I didn't want them to know I've been a jerk today. They think I'm a nice guy. I want to keep it that way." Clive had his hands down in the pockets of his baggy shorts he'd pulled on in the boat to replace the dive suit. "I'm not good with people."

Trevor made a noise in the back of his throat, caught somewhere between scoff and actual half-formed word. He didn't really know what to say. Telling Clive he'd noticed the reluctance to get close to him might suggest there was more going on here than a vacation friendship was a surefire way to never see the guy again.

Hell, it wasn't even a friendship. An acquaintance more like.

Instead he settled for, "How can you own a business that caters to people and not be good with them? The fact you've made a go of it and are quite successful speaks of your ability to be good with people."

"That's business. I can talk all day to tourists and sell them on attractions around the island, give them diving advice, and take them out on the boat, make sure they come back alive. It's all in a day's work. It's the other stuff I have a hard time with."

Trevor waved away the denial. "I saw you the other night with an entire table full of people at the fiesta. They all seemed to know and like you, so I'm not buying this bad with people bullshit." Trevor stopped and turned. He lowered his voice. "If you'd rather I find another person to hang with while I'm on the island, I will. It's no big deal."

If it wasn't a big deal, why did he feel like his heart was going to stop beating and his lungs seize?

Clive ran his hand through his hair. The sun-streaked locks stood up in places. "Maybe that's a good idea."

Trevor clenched his jaw and gave a swift nod. "You got it." He offered his hand in a gentlemanly gesture. "It was nice meeting you. Thanks for the dive, but I really wish you'd let me pay for it."

Clive accepted the gesture and slid his hand in Trevor's, the grip warm and strong. "My treat."

"Thanks. I appreciate it."

Trevor broke the contact before he wanted to and started for the lobby, heart-heavy and soul-sick. If Clive hadn't wanted to at least spend time getting to know him, why in the hell had he invited him to the street fair and then to his bungalow for lunch?

What the fuck did it matter? At least he hadn't gone and slept with the guy after all. Then he'd have felt even shittier than he did at the moment.

That's what he got for thinking someone else could pull him out of the funk he'd been in since he'd come to the island.

Trevor continued forward. He didn't look back, didn't want to know if Clive had started back down to the kiosk relieved that Trevor had stopped following him around like a puppy that had been abandoned on the beach—though he'd always been invited to tag along; he'd never pushed himself into those situations. Which kind of irritated and chafed at Trevor's pride.

For the life of him, he couldn't imagine what he'd done wrong except to say how much he admired Clive for being able to break away from the corporate world. How could that have been taken wrong? Most guys loved it when they made someone envious of their lifestyle. At least that was Trevor's experience.

He went straight up to the front desk to ask about tours to the other side of the island and the abbey. Maybe he'd find a museum or two. If not, he'd take the shuttle boat over to the mainland and see what amusements that part of Brazil had to offer.

A dark-haired girl with bright blue eyes and a nametag that read *Marlie* approached him as he stood looking at a stand of brochures printed in several languages.

"Hi, remember me?"

It took him a minute, but he did place her. She was a friend of Clive's. "Yes. How are you?"

"Good. You went out on a dive today, right?"

"Yeah. To the galleon." God, he didn't want to make small talk at the moment. He just wanted to grab some brochures, make a tentative itinerary for the next few days, and get the hell away from the resort. Given the fact Clive ran his business out of the resort marina and had friends all over the area, it was probably best if he took a few days trip to other parts.

"So you and Clive?"

Trevor's face heated. Marlie really believed in coming straight to the point. "Nope. Sorry. He's a great tour guide, though."

Marlie's face fell. Disappointment clouded her blue eyes. "Don't you think he's hot?"

Trevor laughed. "Very hot."

"Then what's the problem?" She waved a hand up and down him. "I mean look at you. If you were straight, I'd have thrown myself at you that first night."

Trevor cocked his head. Stunned. "How did you know I'm not?"

"It was all in the way Clive was looking at you when you two were at the bar." She stared off into space dreamily.

Trevor laughed. "I think you may be a hopeless romantic."

"It's true. But you can't blame a girl for trying, or wanting to see her friends happy."

"No. You certainly can't." He tapped the brochures he held against his opposite palm. "Well, I have some reading to do and to figure out my plans for the next few days. I'll see you around."

"Sure."

Talk about bad timing. Marlie's attempts to matchmake were about a day late and a dive short. There wasn't anything else to do about it but make the most of the rest of his stay. Of course, he could cut it short and head back to the States and see a little of the US. It had been a long time since he'd gone anywhere outside of New Jersey for longer than a short business trip.

Now that he was recertified he could take a dive tour in Florida, California, or any number of locations. It was something to consider.

He headed to the outdoor restaurant and got a table. Might as well grab some lunch while he looked through the brochures. It was better than hiding in his rooms and letting disappointment and self-recrimination set in. He'd had enough of that in his belly to last the rest of his life and into the next.

The sun began to fall lower into the sky. Sunshine warmed his back and shoulders through his clothes. His face felt hot to the touch. A cool breeze blew in off the water, creating a delicious chill along the perspiration at his hairline.

He gazed around the open restaurant. It really was a nice place to stay. From his vantage point, he could see a good distance from the resort. The bluff where Clive's bungalow stood only looked like a stone's throw. On the hill stood the ruins of what the brochures said was the abbey.

The history of the abbey along with a brief line about the end of a tragic love within the cloistered walls was mentioned on the glossy pages. How could he resist that? Knowing Rodrigo and Juanita's supposed story and having seen the ship Rodrigo sailed, he had to see the abbey where it all ended.

After lunch he returned to his room and grabbed a shower, then changed into different clothes. There was still time to go up to the abbey and look around.

He slipped on a pair of shoes and started out the door, but his phone vibrated on the dresser. How was it that he'd even forgotten to put it in his pocket? Damn sun had gotten to him.

A picture of a horse's ass showed on the screen.

Not Thompson again.

He rejected the call and slid the phone into his pocket. Last person on Earth he wanted to talk to at the moment. Probably another butt dial anyhow. If it was really important either Geoff or Trisha would be the one to call. Since he hadn't heard from them, he'd consider it a nonissue.

Instead of taking one of the shuttles, he decided to walk the distance to the ruins. A bad idea as it turned out. The terrain was uneven in places and the trail grown over. He took a side trail that looked a bit better maintained.

Rocks dotted the uneven ground as the hill swept upward. Vines stretched across the trail, little booby traps of vegetation. He didn't know what they were called, but they were slippery when tread on. He hit a leaf just wrong, not expecting it to be hiding a large rock. His shoe lost traction, and he came down hard on his knee.

He sat there for a moment looking up at the canopy of trees, trying not to toss his lunch. Pain shot stars behind his eyes. He rolled over onto his side, holding his injured knee in his hands. The fucking thing was already beginning to swell. Damn.

It took a moment to get back on his feet. When he did, it was a slower climb up the hill to the road that led to the ruins. He was hot and tired, and his kneecap was busted up like a kid's.

Also, a bottle of water wouldn't have gone amiss. Totally stupid of him to leave the resort without one. The walk was a lot longer than it had appeared while sitting at the restaurant overlooking the resort.

It was another half mile up a winding drive to the abbey ruins. A sign hung across the gated area giving hours for tours. This was apparently not one of them. However, the graveyard attached to the property was open all hours.

Well, why not? He'd made the trek all the way up the hill and lost blood on the way; he might as well make it worth his while and see who was buried on the site.

Grave markers were set at varying angles and spaces. There seemed to be no rhyme or reason to the scheme. The plots were well maintained, other than the headstones showing the signs of weather and erosion. Some of them were so old the letters and dates no longer showed. Placards had been placed at the foot of each grave marker with the names of who had been buried there. Most of those laid to rest were sisters of the order. Their markers were small bricks, humble and unadorned.

Bigger, more elaborate headstones marked the graves of what Trevor assumed were local dignitaries dating back to the founding of Santa Juanita. The money behind the island? Perhaps. It was hard to tell since the placards were in Spanish and Portuguese. Still, some dates were from almost two hundred years ago.

He walked from grave to grave, wondering about the lives of those who had lived on the island and what it had been like back then. If the desolate expanse that remained at present was any indication, it had been pretty barren of both people and structures. Was there anything on the spot where the resort now stood? He'd have to look into that—it might be interesting to delve into local history.

What he really wanted to see were the graves of Rodrigo and Juanita. So far he hadn't found them among the stones. It was probably as he'd suspected and was a legend all along. Also, given the fact at least one of them was a suicide, they would not have been buried in consecrated ground no matter how much the locals pitied and adored them.

That thought just depressed the hell out of him.

A story to remember them by, but no marker to visit.

Pain lanced through his heart.

How long had it been since he'd been to Upper State New York to visit Jason's grave? Two, three, maybe four years already. God in heaven, time had a way of slipping away from a person. He never had any time to go up there and put flowers down or pay his respects.

Trevor had been so angry when Jason's parents had taken him all the way up there to the ass-end of nowhere to lay their son to rest. Granted, that's where they lived and worked, but Jason's life had been in the City. He'd often said he'd never wanted to live anywhere else.

Trevor hadn't spoken to Jason's parents since the funeral. After the burial he'd jumped in his car and returned to their apartment alone, wondering how he was ever going to go on and wishing he'd died.

For some reason Trevor needed to see Rodrigo's and Juanita's graves side-by-side. To know that at least one ill-fated couple were together in death.

Damn, he was getting more melancholy and melodramatic the older he got, but it was a feeling he couldn't shake.

The sun was hanging lower on the horizon. It was time to head back, or he'd be trying to navigate through the trails in the dark without a flashlight or water.

He started back around the property to the main road. Birds called from the trees. Insects buzzed by his ears, and sweat rolled down his back in a steady trickle. It was hot as hell. Not regular heat, but that damn tropical heat that was thicker than syrup and made it hard to breathe.

Off in the distance, thunder rumbled.

Great. Just freaking great. He was going to get caught in a storm.

Trevor looked heavenward and shook his head with a smile lingering on his lips. At some point the only thing left to do was laugh.

He started through the woodsy trails. Switchbacks and hook turns along with the growing darkness in the dense foliage made it hard to recognize any of the surroundings. Had he come this way before?

It didn't seem like it.

How could a trail go uphill both ways? He'd climbed going to the ruins. Shouldn't he be going downhill now?

He stopped and looked behind him, debating whether or not to turn back and find the main road again. Maybe he should have stayed on that instead. It probably would have been more direct, and he wouldn't have gotten lost. Unfortunately that way also led straight past Clive's bungalow, and no way in hell did he want to be seen anywhere near Clive's house.

He continued on.

Thunder grew closer. Lightning started to flash above the tree canopy.

There weren't any places to use as shelter once it started raining. He'd have to pray like hell he got at least close enough to the resort to make a run for it. It wasn't so much the getting wet part that bothered him as much as the wet with electricity flying through the air. That was a recipe for disaster.

The trail twisted around again and put him right back out on the main road. He looked back over his shoulder. Now he was going to get wet and be a target for lightning bolts. At least when he was under the tree canopy he felt somewhat safe, even if it was all illusion.

He started to jog down the sloped road, hugging the shoulder. Each movement of his knee brought fresh pain jarring through the joint. He'd hurt it good when he'd fallen.

A bend in the road curved right in front of Clive's bungalow. Both man and bird were standing on the porch as if waiting for him to pass by.

Determined to keep moving, he quickened his pace, lungs hurting, knee burning.

"Trevor. Come inside. It's going to storm. You don't want to be out in this!"

No, he didn't. But he didn't want to be where he wasn't wanted either. He'd take his chances in the elements. It was a hell of a better proposition than imposing on a man who'd decided he didn't want anything to do with him. And fuck it, here he was limping by on a bad leg like an injured stalker.

Some days really did suck more than others, and this one had turned into a lulu.

Chapter Eight

CLIVE STEPPED out onto his porch. He loved a good storm, especially when his mood was already as foul as the sky. And judging from the speed with which it blew in off the ocean, it was going to be a bad one.

Echoes of footsteps pounded down the road as a runner came into view. Who would be out jogging on an afternoon like this?

Oh shit. Stupid tourist mistake.

"Stop, Trevor. You're going to drown once the rain starts."

Trevor kept going. He didn't even really acknowledge that Clive had spoken, just glanced over with a cutting glare and kept running.

Damn. That was all Clive's fault. Well, he wasn't going to let the guy get caught in a torrential downpour when there was shelter close at hand.

Clive reached up and touched Rodger's foot. "Hold on, buddy. We have to go after him."

Rodger shifted accordingly, but for once he kept his beak shut.

There was something wrong with Trevor's gait. He held his one leg stiffly and almost dragged it along, like his knee bothered him. What the hell had happened to him? The man needed a babysitter or at least a bodyguard.

Clive closed in and grabbed Trevor's arm. "Stop, man. This isn't safe. Plus, you're hurt."

Trevor's knee buckled. They both went down in the dirt. Rodger let out a cry of distress and fluttered his wings.

"Man down!"

"We can see that, Rodger." Clive rolled to sit up first. Dirt was imbedded in his shorts and a long scrape had bloodied his leg from right above his knee to his ankle.

Trevor was much slower to recover. He breathed heavily, his handsome face pulled into a grimace of pain. "Is that what you do when people don't pay attention to you? You knock them down?"

"That was an accident." Clive picked up Rodger and ran a hand over his feathers, then reached down to offer Trevor a hand up. "Come on inside before the rain—" The downpour started as hard and unforgiving as he'd feared. Fire hoses didn't have the force of the rain when it hit.

Trevor rolled to his feet and followed Clive at a fast limp. Now that Clive saw him from the front, he noticed the banged-up knee and swelling along the edges of the kneecap. Christ, that had to hurt.

Clive held the door open as Trevor dragged his leg through. "Come on into the bathroom. We'll clean up in there." He placed Rodger on the back of the couch and showed Trevor the direction.

Clive put the toilet lid down. "Have a seat and let me look at that knee."

Trevor nodded in the direction of Clive's leg. "Yours doesn't look so good either."

"It's just a scratch. What happened?" Clive tentatively touched the puffy area on Trevor's knee, making him suck in a breath and wince. "Sorry."

"It's probably a bad sprain. Nothing a little ice and elevation won't cure." Trevor poked at the area himself.

Right, the man was trained as a physician, and here Clive was on his knees trying to give him advice on his injury. Heat crept up to his cheeks and along the back of his neck. He rubbed the hot spot with his hand.

"Maybe you should wash the dirt off first and see what's what." It was a suggestion, but in no way medical advice. "Look who I'm telling that to."

Trevor glanced up from studying his leg. "What?"

"Nothing. Let me get you a washcloth and some soap." Clive put words to deed and grabbed the stuff he needed, then turned. "You know what? Just grab a shower. I'll go make us something to drink and fix you an ice pack."

Trevor slid his gaze from Clive's and looked back down at his leg. "This is fucking embarrassing."

"What is? The fact you fell?"

"No. The fact I purposely used a trail that wouldn't come out on the road by your house, and I'll be damned if it didn't dump me here anyway." He raked a hand through his hair. "I promise I was only trying to make it back to the resort before the storm hit."

Shame twisted in Clive's gut. This was his fault. He'd made a freaking mess of things. "You don't have to hike miles out of your way just to avoid going by my house. The road out there is free for anyone to use."

"I just didn't want you to think I purposely came by here. I was actually up at the ruins, only to figure out once I'd hiked there that the abbey was closed." Trevor levered himself up by holding on to the sink. He took the towels from Clive. "Just my luck."

Clive swallowed down the rising acid. "We look about the same size. Close anyway. I'll go grab you some dry clothes."

Trevor shook his head as if to say *oh well*. "You've done too much already."

"Don't be a martyr. You can't put your wet clothes back on. That's just being stubborn."

When the silence stretched out, Clive took his leave and closed the door. He leaned his forehead against the cool wood.

He had a lot to feel bad about. Trevor was a good man. A bit hangdog and sad, but a really good man. So unlike a lot of the men Clive had been with over the years. The ones who came and went in his life.

God, he loved that freedom and variety, but seeing Trevor—spending time with him and seeing him as a person, not a plaything—had Clive feeling things he hadn't wanted to ever again. Made him wish for things out of reach. By protecting his own heart, he'd broken another's, and he wasn't so big of an asshole to brush that off.

Sounds from the shower filtered out to where Clive stood. Desire licked at his insides imagining Trevor in there peeling off his wet clothes and climbing under the spray. Lather sliding down a tanned, tight torso to get caught in the nest of springy curls around the base of his shaft.

Holy mother of Santa Juanita!

What he wouldn't give to be in there right now, soaping up Trevor's back and working his way down.

Clive's cock began to stir with arousal. His heart beat hard against his ribs. Breath fanned out along the door. He still hadn't managed to step away.

Suddenly the door opened. Clive grabbed the doorjamb to keep from falling through the opening. Trevor stood there wrapped in nothing but a towel.

It must have been something in Clive's expression. Desire flared between them. Clive wasn't sure who moved first. The only thing he knew was one second he stood there staring at Trevor, and the next he cradled his face and their mouths were fused, tongues swirling.

Trevor's hands gripped Clive's shirt and tugged it out of his shorts. He moaned at the feel of Trevor's hands making their way up his back, along the length of his spine.

Trevor broke off the kiss. "This is going to end badly."

Clive nipped at Trevor's lips. "Probably."

Air puffed out against Clive's mouth as Trevor laughed. "You seem all right with that."

Clive swallowed and studied the gorgeous eyes he'd seen in his sleep since meeting Trevor. "No. I'm not. But it's what we have."

Trevor pressed his lips together and gave a nod. He didn't muddy the moment with words, but simply began to unbutton Clive's shirt and skim it off his shoulders. The hot press of Trevor's mouth against his throat elicited a moan from deep inside. There was nothing rushed or harsh in the action. Trevor's lips were warm and gentle.

Christ, talk about drowning. Clive was about to go down the hard way and all without the aid of tanks or regulator. He slid his hands down Trevor's chest and along the hard planes of his abdomen. Behind the towel, Trevor's cock tented the fabric, proving he needed and wanted this just as much as Clive.

He leaned forward and whispered in Trevor's ear. "You aren't going to call a halt this time, are you?"

"No." The word was hot, solemn, and followed by a tug on the top button of Clive's shorts.

It was taking too long. He just wanted to feel Trevor's naked body pressed against his.

"Hot damn!"

Clive cursed under his breath and stepped into the bathroom, then closed the door. "Damn nosy parrot."

Steam painted the surfaces in a wet sheen. The mirror had fogged over, and the tile floor was a bit slippery.

"You like it hot." Clive gave Trevor a smile and continued to back him up to the shower stall. "If it gets much hotter, neither of us will be able to breathe."

Trevor already looked as if he was out of breath. That made Clive smile wickedly. This was going to be so good.

Clive finished taking off his shorts and stepped out of them, then kicked the garment aside. His shoes followed.

He stood naked in front of Trevor, waiting for either praise or approval. He got neither. Not verbally. Trevor leaned forward and brushed his fingertips along Clive's collarbones—a gentle touch as if trying to get a feel for his skin. Oddly the caress felt more intimate than if Trevor had gone down on his knees and taken Clive into his mouth. Then he leaned in and took Clive's mouth again.

Oh God, he loved this—feeling as if he were the one being seduced. It didn't happen that often. Clive usually came on as the aggressor, pursuing a lover and then getting what he wanted. Most men were happy to give him that control. Clive got what he wanted, and they got a happy memory of the island.

Not this time.

This time he was going to sit back, enjoy, and let Trevor do the work. He might have assured Clive he wasn't going to call a halt, but that was far from a guarantee. This way they'd only do what Trevor felt comfortable with, and it had to be enough this first time.

Trevor unwound the towel from his waist and let it drop. He was even better in the full flesh. He was beautifully proportioned in every sense of the word. Clive drank his fill of the sight before him, his breath catching a bit.

"I don't know about you, but I really want to get this dirt off me." With that, Trevor stepped into the shower and under the spray.

Clive followed, taking up a place on the far side of the stall. It wasn't a big shower by any stretch of the imagination, and having them both inside together posed a logistical problem. Nothing a little soap and careful maneuvering wouldn't help, but neither of them were small men.

He watched in fascination as Trevor soaped up the washcloth and started to run it over his body. Little bubbles clung to his chest in very interesting places. They sluiced down the front of his six-pack like a bobsledder on a hilly course. The glob of foam landed in Trevor's dark pubic hair. The erection stuck out and up, calling for attention.

Unable to watch the show a moment longer without some audience participation, Clive stepped forward and took the cloth from Trevor. "Here, let me do that."

Trevor gave him a smile that lodged somewhere deep in Clive's belly. His cock jerked in reaction. Trevor looked down, and his smile broadened.

Trevor picked up the soap and worked up lather with his hands as Clive started to run the cloth over Trevor's body. Things went from slow and seductive to all-out full-blown sex in a matter of seconds.

Trevor gripped Clive's cock, pumping him in deep strokes that had Clive's eyes rolled back in his head and his mouth open to draw air. Damn that steam. He knew it was a bad idea to leave the shower running so hot. The air was thick and wet. Hard to take into the lungs, but for the life of him, he didn't want Trevor to stop. He didn't even want him to slow down, let alone move to adjust the tap.

"Right there, Trev. God, that feels good."

Clive braced his legs farther apart for support and kicked his hips forward into Trevor's pumping hand. Trevor leaned in, biting at Clive's nipple, sending jolts of pleasure down to his balls.

Clive moaned and bent his head back, resting it against the shower wall. He closed his eyes, trying to drive back the need to come. If this lasted the rest of the night, he'd not complain a bit.

Trevor moved and grunted in pain.

Clive opened his eyes and reached out a hand, grabbing for Trevor should his knee give out. "Maybe we should concentrate on getting clean, then finish this in bed."

Trevor's gentle smile opened a crack a mile wide in Clive's heart. "Sounds like a pretty damn good idea. I don't know how much longer this leg is going to hold up."

Clive took the soap and began to wash himself. Trevor followed his lead and worked on getting clean. It was best this way. If they tried to wash each other, they'd never get out of the shower, and they'd risk injury to both of them.

They finished in record time and dried off.

Clad in towels, Clive helped Trevor to the bedroom. The knee looked even worse than it had when they'd first gotten to the bungalow.

"Shit man, you need that ice pack and elevation more than you need a blow job."

Trevor lay on the bed, leaned against pillows. He felt around the edge of the swelling. "I don't know about that."

The admission was a punch to Clive's gut. Trevor looked like ten kinds of sin sitting there wearing nothing but a towel and tight abs. Minus the knee. That looked painful as hell.

"I'm going to go make that ice pack. Try and get comfortable."

Clive cut through the living room and headed for the kitchen.

"Do you know the way to San Jose...."

Clive turned around. "Jesus, Rodger. I'm sorry, buddy. I forgot I set you on the couch. You want to go on your perch?"

"Hell yes!"

"All right." He picked up Rodger and carried him to the perch. "Here's some seeds."

"*Bon appétit.*"

Clive scratched Rodger behind the crown as the bird dug into the seeds. Now that Rodger was settled, he finished the task at hand. The ice pack was under the kitchen sink. He scooped out ice from the bag in the freezer and poured some inside.

Rain continued to pelt the house. Sounds from outside suggested the storm had intensified. That must have been one hell of a front moving through, because storms usually crossed the island in a matter of minutes before heading back out to sea.

Wind rattled the windows in their frames and howled over the roof. He'd be lucky if he didn't lose tiles up there before it was over. No matter if it let up now or not, Trevor wasn't going back to the resort tonight no matter how much he begged.

By the time Clive got back to the bedroom, Trevor had his leg stacked on several pillows and his eyes closed. Clive stood there, undecided if he should plop the ice pack on the guy's leg or let him sleep.

"Are you going to stand there all night, or are you going to give me the ice pack?"

"I thought you were asleep."

"No. Resting my eyes. Honestly my knee is really starting to throb now. I doubt I'll be able to sleep much."

Clive set the pack down on Trevor's knee. "I'll go get you something for pain."

Trevor's mouth curled into a self-deprecating smile. "You're probably wishing you had let me keep on running."

"No. Not at all." He left the room again and went back into the bathroom to raid the medicine cabinet.

Clive had a lot of wishes at the moment, but to have let Trevor keep running wasn't one of them. He should have never let him walk away that afternoon in the first place. It had seemed such a good idea at the time—to not get involved or in too deep. All it took was to see him running to beat the storm with a bum leg, and Clive had been a goner. Good intentions shattered.

Clive grabbed a bottle of ibuprofen along with an elastic bandage and went back to the kitchen for some water. He returned to the bedroom and sat down next to Trevor. "Pills, water. Do you need anything else?"

"An X-ray, but I doubt you have that here."

"I don't, but no telling what Rodger has stashed around here." Clive smiled at his joke. He was trying to lighten the mood, but judging from Trevor's expression it fell flat. "Are you serious about the X-ray?"

Trevor waved it away. "No. We'll see how it looks in a day or so." He held up his hand. "Don't worry, I won't crash here that long. I'll get down to the resort in the morning."

Clive's heart sank. "Listen, you're welcome to stay here as long as you like. I'm not about to ask you to leave when you can barely walk."

"I'm imposing."

"You're injured."

"I'll survive."

"Yes, but there's no sense in moving until the swelling goes down. You'll only hurt yourself worse." Clive started off the bed again. "Would it help if you wrapped it?"

"Sure."

Clive reached behind him and grabbed the elastic bandage. "Here you go."

Trevor smiled. "You'd make a decent medic."

"No thanks. I like my job, but they are looking for a resort physician to take care of people who need a little more care than over-the-counter meds can provide."

Trevor's mouth curled down at the corners. "I left that part of my life behind for a reason."

"I wasn't suggesting anything. Only making conversation." Clive did wonder why Trevor had turned his back on medicine. Whatever the reason, it didn't seem a happy one or even a career change of heart. It ran much deeper than that.

"If it makes you feel better, I did keep up on my credentials. It was my parents' suggestion. They didn't want to see all their money thrown away if I changed my mind." Trevor wrapped the bandage around his knee as he talked, pulling tight, wincing with every layer. "Fuck." Pain leached the color from his face.

"Are you sure you're going to be all right? Passing out ibuprofen and bandages exhausts my knowledge of joint injuries."

"I'll be fine. It just hurts like a bitch."

"This is going to put a damper on the rest of your vacation."

Trevor secured the end of the bandage with a determined tug. "Not even a little bit."

Chapter Nine

TREVOR WOKE to bright sunshine filtering in from a skylight and pouring down on him with unbearable heat. Where the hell was he?

He pushed up and immediate pain shot through his leg, jarring both his knee and his memory. He was still at Clive's.

The house was quiet. Not even the ravings of an obscene parrot colored the air.

"Hello?"

No answer came back.

Great. Just freaking peachy. He was laid up in a hot guy's bed, and hot guy was gone. That didn't even make getting up worth the effort. If not for a deep well of self-respect, he'd have rolled over and gone back to sleep.

Clean clothes sat on the end of the bed with a note on top of them. Trying not to jar his leg too much, Trevor reached for the paper and unfolded it.

Here's the clothes I promised. Sorry I had to bail. Make yourself at home.—C—P.S Don't try to get back to resort on your own.

So he was stuck here in a strange house where he had no idea what was off limits and what was not and nothing to do all day but stay put and keep his leg elevated. Right. Not going to happen.

Staying put was probably the prudent thing to do under the circumstances, but it damn sure wasn't the most enjoyable.

He swung his leg off the bed, gritting his teeth as the pain throbbed through his knee, then subsided to a dull ache. A dull ache he could manage. It just hurt because he'd slept in one place all night and hadn't moved. Damn, he must have been more tired than he'd thought.

Clive must have been ready to rival Rodger for the profanity awards when Trevor slipped off into sleep without so much as finishing the hand job he'd started in the shower.

Trevor tried not to think about the rumbled sounds of pleasure that had come from Clive's throat, or the way he bucked his hips forward as Trevor pumped him. That was twice they'd started something they didn't finish. One more strike and Trevor was out.

He dressed in Clive's clothes. The shirt fit him fine, but the shorts were snug, even though they were cut a little on the baggy side. Clive was taller and leaner through the waist than Trevor. He decided to leave the button undone for comfort, and headed to the kitchen.

Surprisingly enough his leg didn't hurt too badly to bear weight. It was the side-to-side or rotation of the joint that hurt.

His stomach let out a loud growl. He needed to eat something before he took more medicine. The cupboards and refrigerator were a little on the barren side, but there was some frozen pasta and tomatoes. He'd have to make a quick dish. However, eating Clive's food felt too much like stealing from the guy.

Guilt swam in his belly. If he could get down the hill, he'd be able to grab something to eat at the resort.

It was going to be one hell of a walk downhill, but if he took his time, he'd be able to manage it. He found his shoes and slipped them on, bracing himself for the pain when he bent his knee. Whew, not as bad as he thought it would be.

With hand on the doorknob, he stopped and picked up a piece of paper and found a pen. He wrote a quick note to thank Clive for his hospitality and the clothes. As an afterthought he left his room and cell phone numbers.

He placed the note on the bedside table and left.

The walk down the hill was bad. He'd lied to himself. There was nothing for it. Each step hurt worse than the last. Foliage covered the side of the road. Trevor stayed to the small shoulder and held onto the branches, using them to help support his weight.

Sweat beaded and ran down his face and back. The waistband of the shorts was saturated, and the shirt stuck to his skin. The rain hadn't cooled it off any. It had plunged the area into a steam bath.

A large boulder sat at the edge of the road. Trevor took the opportunity it presented and sat down to rest for a moment. He was a fit guy, but this was ridiculous. Nothing like an injury and stupid center-of-the-sun heat to make a guy feel like a pussy.

Fuck that.

He stood again and stiffened his leg. It was much easier to walk by swinging it out to the side and not bending the knee joint. He was also able to move a bit faster coming down the hill to the straightaway.

The road curved and the resort came into view. Not much farther to go and he could go to his room, shower, and grab some food.

A person on a bicycle came in to view. Not just any person, but one with a parrot riding shotgun in a basket up front.

Busted.

Trevor knew the moment Clive spotted him. Clive's jaw tightened, and he slowed down to a stop beside him.

"I was just coming to check on you."

"Needed something to eat and felt weird raiding your stash."

"You look like shit." Clive leaned over and brushed the hair at Trevor's temple. The sweet gesture unfurled the unspent heat from the night before, even if it came on the edge of an insult.

"I don't think even you'd look good under the circumstances." Trevor backed up a step and leaned against a tree for support. "Though I have a hard time imagining it."

"You want a ride back to the resort?"

"On your bike? With you and the bird?"

"Rodger's the navigator."

"Should have seen that one coming." Trevor laughed and eased away from the tree. "All right. I'll take you up on the offer."

Pride sometimes had to take a backseat to expediency. The sooner he got back to the hotel, the better he'd feel. At least Clive wasn't pissed off that he'd been abandoned.

As Trevor got on the bike, Clive leaned forward, his mouth touching Trevor's ear. "At least do me a favor and order room service. I don't want you to go walking around the hotel on that bum leg. You'll only do more damage."

Trevor couldn't argue with the truth, so he didn't. "Are we going to be too heavy to both be on your bike? We aren't exactly kids here."

The last time he'd ridden a bike like this was probably in middle school when his friend, Benny, used his bike to pull kids along on their skateboards. Trevor and Benny had taken turns pedaling. They kept going up and down the street all afternoon, until the nosy neighbor across the street, who had a moral hatred for kids having fun, came out and made them stop. Later that night, Trevor and his friends snuck out and egged her house.

He smiled at the memory. It was nice to know that all his memories weren't painful. Some were pretty damn good, even in the context of schoolboy high jinks.

The bike tires sunk down into the hard-packed ground as Trevor climbed aboard. The ground, softened by the rain, squished, leaving a trail in the dirt. The extra weight on the back of the bike didn't seem to bother Clive as he began to pedal.

"You all right back there? Try to keep your leg up a little higher as we go into the turn."

Trevor lifted it as the road curved onto the paved lot of the resort. For some reason the thought of Butch and Sundance filtered through his mind along with the song "Raindrops Keep Falling on my Head."

Jason had loved old movies, and that had been one of his favorites.

Trevor pushed the memory away. He'd done too much thinking of Jason over the past week. Too much mourning that should have happened eight years ago.

Clive pedaled them straight to the front lobby of the resort and glided to a stop. He held the bike still while Trevor climbed off. "Let me leave this with the concierge, and I'll help you up to your room."

He lifted Rodger out of the basket with one hand and eased the bike through the side door with the other. Trevor limped along in their wake.

"Rafael?" Clive called out. The rest of the exchange was carried out in rapid Spanish.

Rafael took the bike and put it in a room behind the concierge desk. A few more words were exchanged, but Trevor didn't stay to try and make out the conversation. Upstairs was a shower and bed with his name on it.

Clive caught up to him and swung an arm around Trevor's waist. "Lean into me, man. Don't put any weight on that leg."

"Who's the doctor here?" Trevor snapped, then felt immediately bad about it. "Sorry. I know you're only trying to help."

"No offense taken."

Clive's mouth was very close to Trevor's as they stopped at the elevator. On impulse, Trevor leaned in to brush a grateful kiss across Clive's lips.

A low growl rumbled up from Clive's throat. "What was that for?" The words were sexy, deep.

"Thank you."

The doors opened, and Clive helped Trevor into the car. When the doors were closing, Clive returned the kiss in a not so innocent fashion.

"What was that for?"

"You're welcome."

WHILE TREVOR showered, Clive took it upon himself to order room service for them both. Rodger stood on a towel draped across the back of the chair at the balcony doors. A cool breeze off the water ruffled his feathers. He hummed happily into the wind.

The water in the bathroom shut off. Damn, he'd hoped Trevor would spend longer in there than just a quick cleanup. He wanted the room service cart to arrive *before* Trevor finished.

Trevor limped out of the bathroom, holding a towel closed at the waist. Water droplets dotted his shoulders, making Clive's mouth hunger to play dot-to-dot with his tongue.

Clive cast a glance downward and winced. Trevor's knee was bright purple and black. He'd done it up but good. "That hurts just looking at it."

"Doesn't feel too good standing on it for long periods of time either." He sat down on the bed and lifted the leg up onto the mattress. A gap in the towel gave Clive a vivid shot straight up to paradise, and Trevor's rather large sac.

"You want to wrap that again?"

"In a few minutes. It feels good letting the blood circulate."

Lines crisscrossed and imprinted themselves in a bandage pattern across Trevor's skin.

"You might have wrapped it a bit tight."

"A little." Trevor put his other leg up and leaned back. "I don't even feel like getting dressed. I'm glad you suggested room service. Where's the menu?"

"I already ordered for us. Take it easy. You're on vacation. Nothing you have to do today is pressing."

Trevor gave a bitter laugh. "No. My boss made that quite clear when he forced me to take this trip."

"He was probably looking out for your health, on the whole."

"So says he." Trevor made a face and fell back, defeated, against the pillows. He stretched out his arms in an imitation of a crucified man. "I don't even care anymore."

A knock on the door stalled Clive's question. "Let me get that."

He walked through the suite to the door and opened it. A friend, Phil, stood there, blinking when he recognized Clive. A sly smile slid across his face.

"You staying here now?"

"No. Helping a friend who busted up his knee hiking yesterday."

Concern brought Phil's brow down. "Has he seen a doctor?"

"He is one. And a stubborn one at that." Clive stepped back and allowed Phil to bring the tray inside. "Give me the check. I'm putting this on my tab."

"Good enough for me."

Clive also included a nice gratuity into the total. "Here you go." He shoved the bill and pen back at Phil. "I'll take care of the tray."

"Sure." Phil grinned good-naturedly—more of a sly I-know-what-you're-doing kind of way—then he put the bill to his forehead and saluted as he left.

The first person Phil would tell about seeing Clive in a guestroom was going to be Marlie. Soon after, it would be all around the resort. Not that it mattered much. The resort's general manager, Gaston, was a frequent dive buddy.

Clive pushed the cart back into the bedroom and rolled it close to where Trevor lounged.

"It smells fantastic. What did you get?"

"Nothing special. Spanish omelets and paella."

Trevor's stomach let out a loud rumble. "My stomach says you nailed it."

Clive lifted the covers off the dishes and got everything set up as Trevor maneuvered into a better position.

"This looks really good." Trevor tucked into the meal as if he'd never eaten before. "Oh my God. It's delicious."

Clive grabbed a chair from the desk and took a seat across from him. "Glad you approve. And that you don't have a shellfish allergy."

"No. No food allergies."

They ate in silence for a few moments before Trevor looked up from his plate. "You like taking care of people, don't you?"

Clive had never really considered it, but in the grander scheme he supposed he got some satisfaction out of making sure those he cared about were in want of nothing. He shrugged. "I think most people are like that when they care about someone."

Trevor stalled with his fork halfway to his mouth. "So you care about me?"

Heat crept up Clive's neck and exploded across his face. Years had passed since he'd talked about emotions deeper than a one-night stand. It put him in a very uncomfortable space. "You're an easy guy to care about."

Trevor laughed. "That's a very diplomatic answer."

"No less the truth."

Trevor went back to his lunch, a thoughtful expression on his face. Clive didn't delve into the reason for his contemplative mood. It was better to back slowly away from the conversation as one would a rabid dog or poisonous snake. No sense in getting bitten by something dangerous.

They finished the meal in silence punctuated by random whistles and the occasional song lyric by Rodger. He was just getting wound up to sing a chorus from *South Pacific* when Trevor's phone buzzed on the bedside table.

"Want me to hand that to you?" Clive was already getting up to grab it.

"If there is a picture of a horse's ass on it, leave it. If it's anyone else, I'll take it."

The picture was of a perky-looking female in a power suit. "Says Trisha."

"I'll take that one."

Clive handed him the phone, then sat back down to watch the exchange. Trevor's scowl got worse the longer the call went on. The occasional acknowledgement that someone was speaking broke the silence on Trevor's end, but nothing either way to give an indication of what the conversation was about. Finally he said, "Then drop it."

A startled sound came from the other end, loud enough for Clive to hear it.

"I'm not kidding. At this point the firm is wasting good money. In the long run we'll save more if we build the same or similar product from the ground up."

There was a pause. "Don't think I don't realize that, but hey, he had to be right once in his life."

The call ended shortly after that, with Trevor in a darker mood than he'd been.

"Anything you want to talk about?"

"Work. FDA. Red tape. That about explains the situation in a nutshell."

"Doesn't sound like fun."

Trevor ran a hand across his brow and then the back of his neck. "You know, I was just about to get relaxed for the first time in years— as a matter of fact it's been so long since I've been in a state of *don't care* that I've forgotten what it's like." He paused for a second. "I think I want it back."

"Isn't that what this trip was about? Learning how to enjoy yourself again?"

"Yes. And I came into it under protest. Now I don't think I want to go back to it. At least not that particular job. It's too all-consuming." Trevor made a face and then went back to his lunch. "I still have a few weeks before I have to be back."

"Can I share a little story with you?"

Trevor glanced up. "Please do."

"I went down that same road you did. Climbing the corporate ladder, trying to push myself to the top to garner some kind of outside recognition from people I didn't really like or respect. When I got there—it was a hollow victory. I looked around and decided what I really lived for were my days off. When I didn't have to put on a monkey suit and go into the office and try to impress other unhappy people. It was a turning point."

"That's why you came down here?"

"A bit of it, but not all." No. Clive had come down to outrun a family who turned on him when he'd given up the high life. A family who, for all their wealth, knew nothing but conditional love they only doled out to those they thought were worthy enough to buy it.

He didn't like conditions on affection, especially from his own parents.

"My parents weren't exactly what you'd call warm people, but they looked the other way on my sexual orientation as long as I was successful in the business world and made them look good. It was all about bragging rights with them. Shallow people. Once I quit they decided I was no longer worth their time or emotional support. I was banned from all family functions and contact."

Trevor's eyes rounded and his jaw became slack in surprise. "You're kidding?"

"No. I'm not. My old man was pretty pissed off. The fight that ensued could probably have been heard from space."

That was when true feelings had surfaced, along with a hurtful diatribe that ended in his father blaming Clive's deviant lifestyle—yes, the old man had called it a lifestyle and deviant—on his failure to hold his place at the top. His father had failed to take into account that it was Clive's decision to leave the corporate world. He hadn't been fired.

"Have you spoken to them since?"

"No, nor do I ever plan to. They kicked me out of their lives, so why would I want to have any contact? Let's just say, once I was shamefully unemployed, the gloves came off and I knew their stance on equality and rights was so much politically correct lip service. They never meant a word of it, especially not inside their own family."

Trevor picked up his juice and took a careful sip before setting it back down. "That's awful, man. I'm so sorry anyone has to go through that with their family. I was pretty lucky in that respect. My parents are really cool with it all. Ariel—my mother, and yes, she insists I call her by her first name—is the original Earth mother. A child of the 60s, and all about peace and love. My father—Dan—runs a holistic store in New Jersey and has been in the same location for about forty years now. I don't think they understand my work ethic as far as it consuming my life, but they have never been anything but concerned and supportive."

Clive felt a smile kick up the corner of his mouth. "Yeah, well I guess we can't all be the Cleavers or the Bradys."

Clive took a few more bites of his lunch. The food was excellent, but for all its flavor with the Spanish spices, he could no longer taste it. Years of resentment had a way of ruining even the most delicious of dishes when his thoughts turned to the past. That was one of the reasons he preferred to live in the present.

"The worst part. My boyfriend at the time decided we were no longer good together and dumped me for the guy they promoted into my position when I left."

"Talk about kicking a man when he's down." Trevor's eyes were filled with unbearable compassion and understanding. "Do you think he was only with you for your connections?"

"I've strongly suspected that all these years. Maybe it was coincidence, but I've never believed much in those when it comes to breakups that occur so closely on the heels of a major life change. Feels more like someone cutting their own losses."

"Did you love him?"

Clive leaned his elbows on the table, resting his chin on his hands as he gazed across the meal at Trevor. "At the time, I thought I did. Thought he was the one I wanted to grow old with. After it was all said and done and I moved down here, I realized I had probably been unhappy with both him and the job for a lot longer than I admitted to myself."

Trevor seemed to take that all in, though he made no comment.

"What I'm trying to tell you is that even if you leave that particular job and go do something else, there is always another chapter. Life goes on. Find something that makes you happy and do it. Life is too short to work yourself to death in a job that's making you miserable to begin with. Once you get trapped in that cycle, it's hard to get off, even to save yourself."

Trevor gazed off and out the window. Clive followed his line of sight. A cruise ship was barely visible on the horizon. When he turned back, his pupils were large, eyes soft and full of admiration. "You are an amazing man. I wish I had your balls to chuck it all and start fresh. It's funny, but I didn't realize until the last few days that I haven't even stopped to take a deep breath in the last eight years. It was go, go, go. Push, push, push. I think I overdid that whole 'a body in motion stays in motion' thing."

"Now you have to decide what you're going to do about it, and then just do it. Don't second-guess, don't question, just jump."

Chapter Ten

TREVOR WOKE the next morning to a barrage of phone calls and e-mails, some of them not too nice or subtle. Apparently Geoff had not liked Trevor's estimation of the situation and had told Trisha to go ahead and keep pursuing FDA approval.

It was enough to make him want to tender his resignation. He didn't. Not yet. But he would reserve the right to tell Geoff he told him so when the company was hit with substantial losses, or another company's R & D team did what Trevor had suggested and developed their own product.

His knee was still purple and black, but the swelling had gone down significantly overnight. It was stiff, but not as sore, and could reasonably support his full weight.

Clive had left after a few games of poker and a call from Juan Pablo about something that needed his immediate attention. Trevor hadn't heard from him since.

Sympathy for Clive churned his gut. Who would have guessed by looking at him that he was about as alone in the world as one could get? Not because his parents—family—had died tragically, or because he simply chose to live so far away from them, but because they'd tossed him out of their lives over something as material as money and position.

It was something Trevor had never had to deal with in his entire life. If there was one thing he knew for certain, his parents' love was unconditional. Their support guaranteed. He never had to guess or worry about that aspect of his life. With them he had a firm foundation.

The story had explained so much about Clive, and he'd given the information so matter-of-factly he might have been speaking about an acquaintance. Trevor suspected he did so to hide the exact depth of his pain from people. To find out his parents' support had been a false emotion—well, damn, Trevor had no idea how he'd even have reacted to such a thing. It would have devastated him.

Trevor hurried through a shower, bound his knee, and left his room. After breakfast he walked down to the marina. Clive's boat was not in its slip. At a loose end, Trevor went back up to the lobby and waited on the shuttle that took tourists up to the ruins. He'd try it again, and this time hopefully he'd be able to get into the abbey and look around.

The shuttle wasn't due to leave for another hour, so he walked around the little shops down on the resort's promenade to kill time. Differences in the merchandise at the resort and that found at the street fair in the village were striking. Where the village wares appeared handmade by local artists, the resort sold goods manufactured in bulk and ordered by a buyer. Souvenirs weren't any good unless they actually came from the place visited. Otherwise what was the point in buying something the tourist could just as easily pick up at their local airport on the way into town?

He found one shop at the very end of the lane that had what appeared to be hand-carved goods. In an umbrella stand sitting in the back of the store was a display of hand-carved canes. Trevor picked one up and felt the weight in his hand, leaned on it a few times. The top of it was carved into the shape of a parrot's head that reminded him of Rodger.

A chuckle escaped him. Several shoppers turned to glance at him as if he'd lost his mind. Let them. He didn't have to explain to anyone why he thought it was funny.

He purchased the cane for an exorbitant price that made him blink a couple times, then headed back to the lobby to wait on the shuttle.

Something could be said for walking with a cane. Most people moved and let him go to the front of the line to board the shuttle, though he'd been embarrassed and waved the offer away.

The shuttle rattled up the road to the ruins. It passed by Clive's house. As if an invisible line connected him to the residence, Trevor turned to gaze at the little bungalow as they drove past. A piece of paper was taped to the door, flapping in the light breeze.

The hill tested the shuttle's engine to its limits. How did a resort as expensive and luxurious as this one own a shuttle that was one head gasket shy of disaster? They rounded a corner, and the ruins came into view, accompanied by "Oohs" and "Aahs" from the other tourists.

The shuttle came to a stop in front of the crumbling stairs that led to the front of the main sanctuary. Birds nested up in the corners where the eaves met the partially collapsed roof.

The tour guide stood in front of the group. Trevor had signed up for the tour with an English-speaking guide to ease his understanding.

"There are very few areas of the ruins that are safe. All areas are clearly marked. Please stay within the safety zones and inside the designated walkway." She led them into the ruins.

A good portion of the ceiling was gone, exposing the inside to the elements. Despite the lack of shelter, the inside was swept clean and free of debris. As in the graveyard, there were placards here to describe the different areas and points of historical significance.

The guide gave an overview of the abbey and its founding, information Trevor had already gleaned from the brochure he read. He only half listened to her as he walked around reading the placards and taking in the atmosphere.

It was such a small place, on the top of a mountain, for a few nuns to live so far away from anything and everyone. Faith probably played a large part in their decisions, believing that God had sent them to Santa Juanita for a higher purpose. Unlike Trevor, who had been sent there as a corporate punishment.

Odd how a few days had changed his perspective. Now he didn't feel as much an outcast, but more as if he'd been thrown a lifeline.

They walked through what was left of the small dining hall and the tiny cells where the nuns had slept.

The guide stopped in front of one of the tiny rooms. "This is where Rodrigo Suarez y Rioz spent his last few days on Earth, delirious with fever, not realizing his love had jumped into the sea."

That got Trevor's attention. He looked into the room and was hit with a sense of sadness that seemed to have leached into the very stones of the walls. What a horrible place to come to an end. Only one tiny window allowed any sunshine into the hovel.

"He is buried out on the cliff alongside Juanita Maria de Cortoza. Apart in life, together in death." She turned and made a motion for the group to follow her.

Trevor didn't care about the rest of the tour. He just wanted to wander out onto the grounds to the cliff and see Rodrigo and Juanita's graves. There was something profound there that he couldn't explain, but he knew he'd feel more settled if he could stand at their graves and absorb some of the atmosphere.

Maybe it was because he'd not been to visit Jason's grave in so long that the need nagged at him like a tongue against a sore tooth. He knew he wouldn't leave the island until he stood on that cliff and observed the last view Juanita had seen before taking a plunge over the edge.

Tourists moved past his hampered gait and back out into the sunshine to the graveyard. He let them pass, preferring to take his time and absorb the atmosphere of sorrow and regret.

So much history had played out inside the walls, it was a shame they were allowed to fall into ruin. It might not have been history that rocked the world or even made much difference in the larger worldview, but it had been significant to the island and her inhabitants. That alone made it worth salvaging, or even refurbishing. However, there was a certain mystique associated with half-hollowed out buildings that gave them a sorrowful air and tragic feel. Clive would no doubt say that was what the tourists wanted and expected. Trevor couldn't argue with the sentiment. Look how many people flocked to the Acropolis in Greece, the Coliseum in Rome, and the many castles of the UK.

Billions of tourists passed through those places annually. Stick a ruin on a mountainside or in the middle of a major city, give it a tragic past, and people would come to see it. It was inevitable—people loved a story with a tragic ending.

The thought depressed him as he made his way around the graves he'd seen on his last trip up the hill.

The guide stopped in front of one of the graves. A large, elaborate headstone stood as monument to the deceased's wealth and prominence in Santa Juanita at the time of his death.

"This is the grave of Gutierrez deChamplian. Contrary to legend, he wasn't the villain romantics tend to portray him. Poor Gutierrez was an agent of the Holy Catholic Church who was commissioned by Juanita's father to bring her across the world and into the keeping of the Sisters of the Sacred Madonna. The reason: to keep her out of the hands and marriage of her lover, Rodrigo.

"Distraught that he'd played a part in the tragedy—even as he did his duty—Gutierrez quit the Church in the capacity of agent and lived to serve those who had come to settle on the island. He began to plant crops and build homes and became a father to all who lived here."

Trevor considered the grave, the man, and what Clive had left out of the legend. He had a sneaking suspicion Clive knew the entire story but had amended it a bit to make it more pirate-like. The man—Clive—was nearly a pirate himself. Hell, he already had the parrot. All he needed was the eye patch and a peg leg and he was all set.

He'd probably been one in a past life.

The tour moved on to the cliff and the graves of Rodrigo and Juanita. They were marked by carved stones placed flat into the ground. The placard read that Juanita had stood on that exact spot before she jumped. Though he wanted to trust the story, Trevor had a hard time believing that those who had set the markers knew exactly where she'd stood to take the leap.

When exactly had he turned into a romantic cynic? To pick and choose what parts of the story were true and which were the product of PR? Did it really matter? Probably not in the larger scheme of things.

Trevor moved to the cliff's edge. A small fence provided the only protection against going over the side and suffering a smash against the jagged rocks below. The tide was out at the moment, and the shore pushed back to reveal a line of jetties that curled around the point.

Not even at his most grief-stricken and heartbroken had he stood on a high point and contemplated following Jason into death. Was it because he didn't love him enough? Had he been only fooling himself into thinking Jason was the love of his life, or had he simply possessed a stronger instinct for self-preservation?

If that was the case, why had he buried himself under mounds of work and responsibility, and resisted getting tangled up in another long-term relationship?

Didn't he want to live?

The answer was an undeniable *yes*.

A sexy smile on the face of a handsome man flashed before his eyes. Clive might not want strings or anything permanent, but he had damn sure woken something inside Trevor that could no longer be refused.

He wanted Clive—and before he left the island, they'd finish everything they'd started.

CLIVE STEPPED off the boat, saying good-bye to his chartered guests.

Rodger bobbed up and down in his version of a bow. *"Thank you. Come again."*

The guests laughed, charmed by the bird.

Clive reached up and scratched Rodger's head. "I'm proud of you, buddy. You only cursed once today."

"Jolly Rodger's a good boy."

"He's a very good boy. I think a special treat is called for."

Rodger bobbed faster. *"Hot damn!"*

Clive went to the kiosk to check messages and go over the schedule for the next day.

Juan Pablo shook his head when he saw Clive.

"What?" Clive set Rodger on the counter. He leaned down to grab his phone out of his rucksack. No calls. Damn. He'd hoped he would have heard from Trevor. He needed to go and check on him.

"That guy was here again looking for you." Juan Pablo continued to shake his head. "Whoever he is, he's pissed."

Clive backed up a bit. "What the fuck? Did he say why?"

"No. But he went off on you like you were everything but a good man."

"What's his problem?" Clive came around the counter and stepped into the kiosk. "Did you get a picture of him?"

"No. I was afraid to take my phone out."

"You could have told him you were calling me." Clive picked up the clipboard. "No charters for tomorrow? That's not good."

"There will be. Give it time. The boat from the mainland hasn't docked yet. They're a little late today."

"If not, I'll take a private party out, and we can do some real diving rather than the tourist runs." The thought of getting Trevor into one of the caves to dive made his blood heat as if he'd just drunk a shot of aged whiskey.

Warmth spread through his body. He wanted to show Trevor all the island's secrets and beauties. There were more wonders to behold under the ocean than there were topside. Clive had seen the look in Trevor's eyes behind his dive mask when he'd first seen the galleon. There was wonder, awe, and joy. It was a moment worth remembering, and the fact Clive had given it to him sent a thrill of satisfaction through him.

"Spread the word. If no paying fares, we all go out and make a day of it."

The more he thought of it, the more he liked the idea. It had been a long time since he'd done a tour just for his friends. It was past time to take a day off and enjoy a dive with those closest to him.

"Will do, boss." Juan Pablo tapped a pencil on the counter, which Rodger tried to catch with a foot. "What do you want me to do if your friend comes back?"

It took Clive a moment to realize Juan Pablo referred to the mystery man and not Trevor. "Tell him to wait here, and call me. I'll be right over."

"Got it."

Clive picked up his rucksack and stepped out of the kiosk. He scooped Rodger off the counter and put him up on his shoulder. "Want some lunch, buddy?"

"Tastes like shit."

"I'm sure it won't."

As they walked along the dock, Clive looked up and saw Trevor waiting for him at the top of the stairs. His chest tightened in anticipation. A smile spread across his face before he could check it. There was no help for it. He was starting to get into the guy in all kinds of ways.

The cane was a nice and practical touch. It gave him a rather continental air, even if he was wearing a pair of baggy jeans shorts and a short-sleeved Henley. Trevor still had the injured knee wrapped, and he leaned on the cane as if the leg bothered him.

"I was just coming to check on you." Clive closed the space between them, coming to stand on the landing. "How you feeling?"

"Leg seems better. I picked up a DME at one of the shops on the promenade."

"DME?" Clive raised a brow as they started to walk back toward the hotel.

"Durable medical equipment, though this one is a little more elaborate than the ones my company sells." Trevor lifted it up and turned it to show Clive.

"Oh that's great!" Clive laughed. God, he hadn't felt so good in years. Not when just seeing someone brightened his day and made him happy to be alive.

"I thought of Rodger when I saw it. So far it's the only souvenir I've bought." Trevor set it back down and leaned on it as he walked. "What does that say about me?"

Disappointment rose to squash the bud of happiness. Clive cleared his throat. "It says you don't like taking a bunch of useless junk home with you."

"I should probably get something small for my parents, though. They were kind of surprised I even came here. They'll want proof."

Clive envied Trevor the relationship he had with his parents. How different would his life have been if his parents had actually been worth a damn as humans? Some people shouldn't have children, and they were prime examples. However, if he hadn't left, he wouldn't now be living in paradise and his tiny corner of it. No regrets—it was the mantra of his life.

Trevor stopped at the intersecting hallways where lobby and restaurants split. "What are your plans for the rest of the day? You have another tour to take out?"

"Nothing for this afternoon. What did you have in mind?"

"Honestly, I was thinking of taking a swim and doing some laps in the pool, exercise this knee some, without putting a lot of weight on it." A sensual smile played across Trevor's lips. "I'd love for you both to join me."

"Rodger doesn't swim, but I'll be glad to join you."

"Swimming with the fishes!" Rodger danced around and began quoting random lines from *The Godfather*.

Trevor laughed. "Never a dull moment with him around, huh?"

"You don't even know the half of it."

As they walked, their hands brushed together. Clive had the overwhelming desire to take Trevor's hand in his, but he refrained. It was such an intimate thing, more so to him than having sex. Holding a lover's hand was a sign of true affection. That you cared more about the person than just the orgasm they could give you. It was an entirely different level of intimacy—a higher one as far as Clive was concerned.

He chanced a glance at Trevor. His dark eyes were full of hope and promise. "Do you want to get something to eat first and swim later?"

"Let's swim first. I've been walking around those ruins today and need to cool off a bit."

"You went on the tour?" Clive figured Trevor would venture up there again but had wanted to be the one to take him there.

"Yes." Trevor drew the word out. The heat in his eyes changed to mischief. "I think you left something out of your story the other day. You never mentioned Gutierrez ended up founding most of the island."

"Yeah, well. It doesn't make for as romantic a tale as the villain getting his comeuppance."

Trevor laughed. "Oh, I think he was a tragic figure in his own right. Torn between duty and honor and what he knew was morally correct, that's pretty powerful stuff. Then to pay a penance he left the church. It's a great turn."

Clive placed his hand on Trevor's shoulder, massaging the muscle there. "Should have known the redeemed villain story would appeal to you."

"Why do you say that?"

Clive gave a shrug. "Because you seem the type to root for the underdog."

"Or the guy who's been maligned in the story?"

They started walking again. The sun baked down hot and unforgiving, but a cool breeze ruffled Clive's hair. He was in need of a cut, but there hadn't been time lately. Keeping one hand on Trevor, Clive used the other to push the errant bangs from his forehead.

He liked touching Trevor, to pretend he had a right to keep his hand on him in a tender, yet possessive, manner. Trevor hadn't asked him to remove it or turned in such a way to dislodge it. Instead he limped along the hallway, using his parrot cane on his bad side and smiling like a man who'd just won the hookup lottery.

But this was much more than a hookup. It had been from the start, but Clive was too pigheaded and stubborn to realize it until he'd tried to send Trevor away. Big damn mistake. He'd stood on his porch for hours, trying to think of a way to see him again that wasn't so obvious, so fickle.

Clive's belly let out a loud growl, making Trevor laugh.

"All right, I think I can forgo a swim until we feed you."

They sat in the outside restaurant. Rodger perched on the back of an empty chair and was treated to a bowl of fruit and nuts. He dug into the dish with enthusiasm and a rolling commentary of the offerings.

The meal was long and leisurely, and Clive enjoyed good conversation and a side of Trevor he hadn't thought existed.

"You seem very relaxed today," Clive commented as he leaned on the table over his dessert plate. It was a testament to how far he was willing to go to stretch out the moment if he lingered over sweets. They just weren't his thing.

Trevor gave a reluctant smile, more into his coffee than to Clive. "I saw Rodrigo's and Juanita's graves today and had an epiphany."

"Sounds painful," Clive teased.

"No. It was an eye opener about why I've closed myself off from the world and poured all I am into the job. A living death kind of thing." He gazed off across the water. "Not going to do that anymore. From now on I'm going to do things different, better."

"Glad to hear it. You'll live longer." It was meant as a joke, but as soon as the words were out of Clive's mouth, Trevor's expression changed, hardened.

"And I haven't been living very well lately. I've been existing." Trevor stopped while the waiter came to check on them and leave the bill.

Clive didn't want to pry, but he couldn't help nudging the guy a bit. Talk about a story. He knew Trevor had one—everyone did—but there had to be a deeper reason for his workaholism than just being different from his parents. Not to say his parents didn't work hard, but they sounded a bit better balanced than their son for the work-life ratio.

When the waiter walked away, Clive asked, "Why have you merely existed?"

Trevor stared across the table at Clive. He took off his sunglasses and looked Clive square in the eyes. "Eight years ago my lover, Jason, died in my arms, and it was my fault."

Chapter Eleven

IT WAS one of those moments that happen only in movies. One of the characters drops a bombshell and there is a dramatic pause before everything swings back into motion. At least it felt that way to Trevor.

He sat across from Clive, waiting for the demand for an explanation to come. It never did. Clive gently laid his hand on top of Trevor's.

"I'll get the check, and then we're going up to your room and talk about this. It's never a good idea to open a vein in public."

Trevor's eyes stung. He nodded. What else was he supposed to do, sitting there among people who were enjoying their vacation—and had every right to.

God, he'd so not planned to do this. He hadn't even intended to tell Clive about the past. The plan was to let it lie buried in the grave with Jason. Resurrecting it was the last thing he wanted to do now he'd decided to let it go. But that damn well of emptiness that had tormented him for years had not fully gone away, even with his realization. It remained there, nagging him to explain and tell Clive the most painful details of his life. To make him understand the reasons why he'd shut himself up in an office with piles of work and no personal life.

By silent agreement, they didn't speak again until they'd reached the suite. Even Rodger was unusually quiet. Once inside, Clive perched

Rodger by the window and then came back and sat in the little living room with Trevor. Very close, so their thighs touched.

Clive picked up Trevor's hand as it rested in his lap. The action was so surprisingly tender. For a tough guy, he had some depths of feeling unnoticed until he wanted them seen.

"I assume since you brought it up, you wanted to purge your gut."

Though the situation was tense and Trevor's insides roiled with the knowledge he was about to tell his darkest secrets, he smiled. Clive might have tender feelings, but he expressed them in a plainspoken way.

In these cases the best place to start was at the beginning.

"Jason and I met in college. NYU. We were both undergrads, and it was one of those moments you read about where you meet someone and hit it off immediately. It's clichéd and melodramatic, but true. We had an instant rapport I've never felt with anyone before." He left off the part where he'd felt a similar pull to Clive, sitting in that bar the first night. No need to compare such things at the moment.

"What started as a great friendship evolved into love by our sophomore year."

Clive squeezed his hand, encouraging him to continue.

"Years passed. We moved in together. We were pretty sure we were going to spend the rest of our lives together. I'd finished my residency and had been offered a job at a hospital in New Jersey."

Pain rose into Trevor's chest, threatening to block his air and crush his heart. He kept going. If he didn't get it out now, he wasn't going to.

"We were coming home one night. It was late. We'd been house hunting in Jersey all day and had found one we liked near the hospital where I'd be working. I never saw the attack coming." His voice cracked. Tears filled his eyes. The scene unfolded in his memory as if it were happening right then in front of him, and still he was helpless to react.

"One moment Jason was walking in front of me discussing what he wanted to do to improve the patio should we buy the house, the next I hear a loud pop and Jason is in my arms, bleeding to death."

Clive leaned forward and pulled Trevor into his arms. Trevor had not realized he was sobbing until he felt the wetness on his cheeks.

"How is that your fault? You did nothing wrong." The words were harsh against Trevor's hair, fierce as if Clive meant to protect him from the past.

Trevor clung to Clive, speaking against the tearstains on his shirt. "I couldn't save him. I tried. I tried so hard and he fucking died. What kind of doctor was I, who couldn't even save the one man I loved? How was I supposed to save others if Jason was dead? Why would I even want to?"

The night had been full of noise and confusion. Sirens screamed in the distance. Trevor attempted CPR. A woman from their building helped by pressing her hands over the injury in Jason's chest.

Trevor pulled away from Clive, looking into his face. "It was hours before I ever noticed the blood on my clothes. Then, only when I caught a reflection of myself in the hall mirror when I walked into our apartment. I was so numb I hadn't even noticed."

It ran deeper than that. He'd stared at his reflection as if looking at someone else. Somehow his mind and body had become detached, and he was merely walking through the scene but not really participating in it. His mother, Ariel, had stood behind him with her hands on his shoulders for the longest time—just standing there—ready to offer him comfort or support should he need it.

Clive ran his thumb over Trevor's face, wiping his tears. "Under the circumstances it's understandable. Natural."

Trevor leaned back against the sofa cushions, still in Clive's arms, but now slightly apart. "You know the worst part of that night? Jason wasn't the target. The shooter was aiming for someone walking along the sidewalk by us."

Clive linked their fingers together. "I'm so sorry, man. No one should have to bury a loved one. Not for such an unnecessary act of violence."

Now that the worst of the story was out, Trevor wanted it finished. "After that—after I couldn't save Jason—I quit my job and got hired at Global almost immediately. I worked my way up from sales to the VP office by concentrating on nothing but the job. It was much easier to throw myself into work than to deal with the grief. Jason's death left a huge void in my life, and I couldn't bear it."

Worse, the walls seemed to close in on him whenever he was alone in the apartment. All Jason's belongings seemed to take on a life of their own. His clothes hung in the closet for months, remained in the laundry basket, because Trevor simply didn't have the strength or want to deal with the pain of sorting and separating them.

"It took six months before I moved out of that apartment. When I packed, I packed around Jason's belongings because I couldn't stand to disturb them. Like I would violate some sacred dirty laundry pile shrine if I dared pick up his sneakers or take his jacket off the back of the recliner where he'd thrown it."

Trevor shook his head and ran a shaking hand through his hair. "In the end I had to call his sister to have her come and pack Jason's things while I was at work. I couldn't even stand to be in the apartment when it was done. How pathetic is that?"

Clive put his arm around Trevor and hugged him close. "Everyone grieves in different ways and at their own pace. You chose to deal with it by pouring all your energy into work. It wasn't wrong; it was just your approach."

Trevor shot to his feet and started pacing. Emotion roiled in his chest, stomach, and head in a noxious soup he wanted to purge. "But it was wrong. Don't you see? I hid from life for eight years, keeping myself shut away in an office, living only for a job that did nothing more than keep me going because it was easier to deal with those problems than it was my own. You spotted it the moment you met me, and you had no idea of my story or what I've been through."

Clive's green eyes were soft, caring. "And you've punished yourself enough. Did the coroner's report definitively say that Jason could have been saved? That you didn't do enough at the scene, or should have done something different?"

Trevor hung his head, wiped at his face with his hands. "I don't know."

"What? What do you mean you don't know?"

"I never looked at the report." Jason's parents had sent a copy to Trevor when it was made available. He'd never been able to open it and read the words he knew to be true. He'd missed something and hadn't known—had done what every medical practitioner knew to be true, that it was impossible to work on someone you loved. In his panic and fear, he'd blanked and started CPR when he should have been trying to stop the bleeding instead. Over the years he'd practiced again and again what to do if ever presented with the situation a second time. He would never feel that helpless or afraid again. Never.

Clive let out a pitying sigh and shook his head. "Trevor, you really need to read that report."

"No, I don't. Reading it isn't going to bring Jason back."

"I'm not suggesting it will, but it might lift this guilt you've been living under." Clive leaned over onto his knees, looking up at Trevor. "Think of it this way: would Jason have wanted you to close yourself off from the world, or would he have wanted you to enjoy the life you still have to live?"

Truth rang in the question. Jason would have hated to see what Trevor's life had morphed into. Before Jason's death the two of them were hardly ever home except to shower and change clothes. They were always going off on some excursion, even if it was only a day trip. They may have only been together for eight short years, but they'd loved enough for a lifetime.

Trevor sat and lowered his head to his hands.

Clive rubbed a heavy hand across his shoulders. "You've had what most people only dream of—a love that's pure and true. You didn't have to second-guess it or deal with your partner's bullshit. That's a gift. It's rare and you were one lucky son of a bitch to have gotten that for at least a short time."

Trevor turned to stare at Clive. "Is this a pep talk? Because if it is, you really suck at them."

Clive's hand crept up Trevor's neck. "I don't do pep talks. I tell truths."

"You don't believe in the gentle approach."

"I think that's been used on you once too often over the years. It's obviously not worked. Someone needs to get rough with you."

Despite his miserable state, Trevor laughed. "And you're the man for the job?"

"Always."

CLIVE LET the word hang on the air. Trevor blinked a few times but had no smart or snappy comeback. Clive had never suffered fools lightly, nor allowed them to keep on a destructive bent if he cared for them. And dammit somewhere along the line in the last few days, he'd begun to care about Trevor. The man was a walking mess who only held it together by a shoestring and was too stubborn to even realize it.

Trevor leaned back against the cushions, his hands on top of his head. "I've been whining."

"No. You've been purging. Totally different animal." Clive ached to hold him, and God, he wanted Trevor so bad right now but feared even making a move. What kind of an opportunistic asshole would he seem if he told Trevor that seeing him unburden himself of close to a decade of guilt had gone right straight down into Clive's soul and buried itself there.

Call him a sucker, but there was just something about seeing a strong, capable guy brought to tears that turned him to mush.

Trevor turned to him. "It's been so hard to talk about. Most people want to tell me it's not my fault and to live my life, but no one offered a way to make that happen. Until you."

"Me?" Clive put a hand to his chest. "Hey, even I told you to start living."

"You told me that when I first got to the island. Not after you knew my story." Trevor narrowed his eyes. "You saw right through me."

"Well, I don't know about that, but I did see you were killing yourself with work." Clive shifted on the couch so he fully faced Trevor. "I don't think anyone could have guessed your story, least of all me."

"And see that's the best thing. You knew I was in trouble without even knowing the cause, or how long I'd been living this way." Trevor took his hand and brought it to his mouth, pressing a kiss to his knuckles, then moving to the palm. "You showed me how to live again."

If Clive had been a gentleman he'd have pulled his hand from Trevor's and warned him of how this might not be a good idea under the circumstances. Trevor was bound to feel vulnerable after opening such a deep wound. However, Clive wanted him so much he wasn't going to deny Trevor anything he wanted. Maybe it was just what Trevor needed to live again.

In a case like this, it was best to let the one doing the healing to heal as he saw fit.

Trevor ran his thumb over Clive's hand. "You know, I'm about out of the notion of a swim."

Not one to talk himself out of getting laid, Clive allowed Trevor to pull him forward. "If you're absolutely sure."

"Oh, I've never been surer of anything in my life."

Well, all right. At least he could make love to Trevor with a clear conscience. He'd asked the important question. That was good enough.

Their mouths met, tentatively at first. This was no lovemaking spawned from lust, but from the gentler emotions. Christ, how long had it been since Clive had a gentle lover? Too long. Most of his were hurried bouts of passionate sex with little feeling behind them.

His heart raced, breath came fast. The taste of salt from Trevor's tears put a lump in Clive's stomach. It must have been amazing to be loved so deeply by this man—to be everything in the world to him. A spike of jealousy and envy roared through his blood.

Clive had never once, in all the lovers he'd had, been one man's everything. Not ever. It was a sobering and sad thought.

Clive cradled Trevor's face in his hands and kissed him slow and deep, and then he broke away. There were so many things he wanted to say, but all the words got caught in his throat. Sometimes silence was the better part of valor.

Trevor rose and held his hand out for Clive. "Let's go to bed."

Clive followed Trevor into the bedroom of the suite. Rodger gave a low whistle as if understanding the importance of the moment.

Clive chuckled nervously. "Let me put him somewhere else. He'll do nothing but critique us."

"And that would be weird."

"Yes." Clive moved past Trevor and collected Rodger from the back of the chair. "Sorry, buddy, but we don't need an audience or coach."

"Walk the plank!"

"I plan to."

He set the bird on the minibar and turned on the radio for him. Rodger started bobbing to the music, showing off his moves.

"Rock on, Rodger."

"Salsa!"

Clive went back into the bedroom. Trevor was in bed, clothes folded on the chair.

"Figured I'd get things rolling since you seem a little reluctant at the moment." Trevor lifted the sheet, a clear invitation for Clive to join him.

Trevor was beautifully naked and fully erect. "The only reason I put the brakes on that first night was because I felt a connection to you I hadn't experienced since Jason. It seemed a betrayal."

Clive sat down on the edge of the bed and ran a hand over Trevor's hard belly. He was surprised that his fingers shook. "I understand, believe me."

Oh, he more than understood. He was right there with him on the connection bit. Peel back the layers and they were very similar underneath. More importantly, he didn't think Trevor had it in him to hurt another human being. It wasn't genetically coded into his DNA the way it was most people. He was a decent, stand-up guy. One that if you gave him your heart, he'd protect it with his life if necessary.

Clive ached. Deep. Down in places where he'd never allowed anyone to reach. He really could learn to love this man with very little effort, and the thought both excited and terrified him.

Trevor wound their fingers together and slid them down to touch his hardened shaft. "You can touch me, you know? I won't break."

"Your leg. I don't want to hurt you."

Trevor's cock was hot and thick. Clive's mouth watered at the feel of Trevor so vital and alive in his hand. "I'll stay on the bottom."

A moan purled up into Clive's throat at the thought of taking Trevor—topping him. Later, though, not now. This time he wanted to be gentle and loving. To show Trevor this was something to cherish and not get over in a rush to finish.

Clive leaned over, taking Trevor into his mouth.

"Oh God." The words ended on a moan as Trevor put his hand in Clive's hair, capping his skull. "That feels good."

It *was* good. Giving Trevor pleasure was an easy thing to do. The man was made for worshipping.

Trevor lifted his hips off the bed, coming up to meet Clive's seeking lips and tongue. He was close, Clive could tell. He didn't want him to come yet. Not until they had explored every avenue of pleasure possible.

Clive left off the pursuit and moved upward, kissing a trail toward Trevor's mouth. He was still fully clothed, and the thought of moving over a naked Trevor while still dressed struck him as erotic in ways he'd never dreamed.

Trevor's eyes were dark and hot. "Why did you stop?"

Clive gave him what he knew to be a sexy smile. "Because we've been dancing around this for the better part of a week, and I want it to last. You wanted slow, you got it." He leaned down and pressed his mouth to Trevor's.

The kiss was tender, delicious, and full of promise.

Trevor moved his hands to the bottom of Clive's shirt and spoke against his lips. "I think it's time you had a little less on."

Clive allowed Trevor to pull the shirt over his head. "Is that better?"

"It's more than better." Trevor ducked his head and ran his tongue over Clive's throat. When he came back up to his mouth, he whispered, "You have no idea how good it is."

Oh, but he did. Clive was about to die a thousand sensual deaths. He was even starting to think in poetic terms, and he so wasn't that kind of guy. He was blunt and to the point. He'd never believed in waxing poetic or mixing words. This man beneath him was changing him in ways he'd never thought possible, and he rather liked it. There was freedom to be found in Trevor's arms.

If he could only manage to forget that this was all temporary. Trevor wasn't someone he could keep.

The reminder nearly shattered Clive. He took Trevor's mouth in a savage kiss of longing, desperation, and need. Then admonished himself for the act. He wasn't going to go that route. This was for love.

Trevor surprised Clive by giving back as good as he got. His hands sank down into Clive's shorts, rounding over the crest of his ass and sliding the fabric down. Breeze from the open window cooled his heated skin. His cock throbbed with the need to bury it deeply in Trevor's welcoming body.

He sure hoped the guy brought lube and condoms with him on vacation, because Clive had nothing with him at the moment. It was enough to stall him.

Trevor's heavy-lidded gaze slowly widened. "What's wrong?"

"I hope you brought some supplies in your luggage."

The smile was knowing and sexy as hell. "Yes. I wasn't looking for this to happen when I came down here, but I believe in being prepared."

Clive sent up a *thank you* to the universe. Going down to the gift shop would have been totally out of the question. It would have been all over the resort by sundown.

Trevor leaned over and pulled out a small tube of lube and a box of condoms from the bedside table. "We'll put them within easy reach."

"Good thinking." Once they got going at it hot and heavy, he didn't want to have to stop to fumble around looking for things. It might interrupt his groove.

Trevor looped his arm around Clive's neck. "Are you stalling?"

The idea shocked Clive. He laughed. "No. God. No."

Trevor's eyes twinkled with a teasing light. "Just checking."

Clive grew warm inside. Not from his desire for Trevor, but from a sense that as a lover he was going to be fun.

And if there was one thing in this world that Clive considered his own personal kryptonite, it was a lover who knew how to have fun.

Chapter Twelve

IN BUSINESS, Trevor always knew when he had a potential client or vendor on the ropes. They would get a look in their eyes that said they'd follow anywhere they were led. Clive had that same look on his face, though he was undoubtedly too cool to ever admit such a thing out loud, let alone to himself.

Trevor shook his head in a pitying manner. "You're still wearing too many clothes, man."

Clive lifted his hips and slid his shorts over his firm butt. Not surprisingly, he'd gone commando. His cock stood up from a nest of tawny hair. Few tan lines marred his toned body, which made Trevor wonder if Clive lay out on his bluff in the buff.

Trevor drank in the sight, wishing to memorize every line, angle, and freckle. There was a nice dusting of freckles along the tops of Clive's broad shoulders. "I bet if they put your picture on the tourism brochures, Santa Juanita wouldn't be able to handle the influx of visitors."

Clive lay down beside Trevor. "Doesn't matter."

The words were delivered in a near whisper as Clive started placing little teasing pecks along Trevor's jaw.

Trevor closed his eyes and allowed himself to fall into sensation—to not do anything but feel and react. For each movement Clive made, Trevor made a countermove. It was give and take. Words slid into quiet murmurs and moans of pleasure. They took turns learning each other's bodies and what elicited the best responses.

As far as Trevor was concerned, Clive could do no wrong as a lover. He had a barely contained edge to him, telling Trevor that Clive held back his natural inclination to dominate and go at it hard. This time, for whatever reason, he didn't break the slow and meticulous pace.

By the time Trevor was ready to receive Clive, a sense of being thoroughly and completely loved had settled in the middle of Trevor's soul. This joining was merely the icing on a really great cake.

Clive faced him, staring down into his face as he moved in a slow, maddening rhythm that rocked Trevor all the way to the soles of his feet. Clive had one hand on the headboard of the bed and the other on Trevor's jaw. His thumb brushed tenderly over Trevor's bottom lip as they moved in time.

Trevor looked up into Clive's beautiful eyes. The gold had deepened, the green hot and vibrant. Trevor could happily stare into those eyes for the rest of his life and never grow tired of them.

But it wasn't to be—not now. It was this moment in time and nothing more. Forever was a dream that had a way of turning into a nightmare. It wasn't a place he wished to go—not now. Not when Clive flexed his hips and closed his eyes.

Not when they both sat on the edge, about to fall into the void.

Clive skimmed his hand down Trevor's body, leaving a trail of heated flesh in his wake. When he reached Trevor's cock, he started a slow, sensuous pump with a firm hand. Trevor threw his head back, bucking his hips upward.

Oh man, he wasn't going to last now. Not in the face of this incredible lovemaking. Not when everything inside him was going tight and hard.

Breath passed through his open lips in little gasps. His skin was slick and wet.

Clive let out a soft string of curses in several languages. They fell on the air as proof he held on to control by a very slim thread.

Tiny pulses shuddered through Trevor, proclaiming that Clive had found satisfaction. His hand tightened on Trevor, stroking him until he too came on a whisper of harsh words, as tender thoughts moved through his head.

Several moments passed before either of them moved. Clive rolled to the side and rested on his elbow, looking down into Trevor's face. Trevor turned to study him. The expression on Clive's face was one of sweet surprise.

"Worth the wait?" Trevor ventured.

Clive didn't answer. He simply leaned forward and brushed his lips gently over Trevor's.

"All right. I'll take that as a yes."

Clive just gave him a sexy smile.

Personally Trevor thought it was some of the best sex he'd had in years—since Jason. But then, Jason wasn't about finesse. He had been young, horny, and in love. Style hadn't much mattered to him, or to either of them really. It was different as a mature man. He'd never really stopped to think about it before, but now that he had, he couldn't seem to shake it. Not that it diminished his love for Jason's memory or what they had shared in their youth. Nothing could ever erase the sweetness of that first true love. This was memorable, though. A standard to measure other lovers by.

Clive ran his thumb over Trevor's brow. "You're frowning."

Trevor laughed, embarrassed that he'd been caught thinking way too hard after having what should have been casual sex. Hell, it was anything but casual. It was life affirming. "I was just thinking about Jason."

"Understandable." Clive brushed his fingers through Trevor's hair, turning his face ever so slightly toward him. "You don't have to explain what's going through your mind. You've had a very emotional day."

It had been, but in a cathartic way. "I think he'd approve."

"He no doubt had really good taste."

Trevor smiled. "He had to, right? He was with me after all."

"That stands to reason." Clive slid down onto the bed and laid his head on a pillow. "I think I could sleep for at least a week now."

"Your business is going to suffer."

"I don't think Rodger would let me get away with a week in bed, so no sweat. He'd be screaming for seeds."

As if on cue Rodger belted out, *"I'm gonna wash that man right out of my hair."*

Trevor exploded with laughter. He couldn't help it. That little blue guy had a way of getting to a person and just making them see the world through the uncomplicated eyes of a parrot. Rodger said things that most people only wished they had the guts to. He truly lived in the moment as most animals did, and cared not who knew it.

Clive shrugged. "What can I say, he also likes musicals."

They lay there and talked while Rodger sang random bits of Broadway plays from the other room, competing with the songs that poured through the radio speakers.

Trevor lay in a state of complete happiness, waking up a few hours later, not even realizing he'd fallen asleep. The bed next to him was empty.

Sounds of water came from the bathroom. Clive must have stepped into the shower. No matter how tempting the thought of joining him in there, Trevor just didn't have the steam to move. He was relaxed in a way he hadn't been in a very long time.

Besides, he was on vacation. If he didn't want to move, he didn't have to. Right now, he seriously didn't want to even contemplate doing anything more than breathing in and out. He was sore in places that reminded him how long it had been since he'd had any kind of sexual recreation. His knee kind of bothered him too. However, he wasn't about to admit that to Clive.

The shower stopped. A few minutes later Clive came out, wearing a towel. "You're awake."

"Not really."

"Go back to sleep. I'm going to run and get some food from this killer little restaurant I know. It will only take a little while to get it."

Trevor started to get up. "You want me to go with you?"

"No. I'm going to leave Rodger here. I'll be back."

Trevor made a *come here* motion with his hand.

"What?"

"Come here." Trevor waited until Clive was within easy reach and snatched the towel from around his hips. He sat up and took the flaccid piece into his mouth, feeling it harden quickly as he started to suck.

"I guess the food can wait." Clive capped Trevor's head with his hands. "You do that so well, Trev."

Trevor didn't say anything. It was rude to talk with a mouth full. He kept working Clive over, taking him all the way down into his throat. Clive put his foot up onto the bed and started to thrust his hips forward.

Trevor cupped Clive's balls, squeezing as he sucked.

Then Clive was in motion. He pushed Trevor back on the bed and climbed on top of him, moving so his cock hovered over Trevor's mouth, so he could take Trevor into his own.

Bliss, pure and unadulterated, moved through him as they sucked each other into explosive orgasms.

This was amazing, and it put no pressure on his injured knee. That alone was enough to put it at the top of his list for awesome things he'd done on his vacation.

Trevor ran his hands over Clive's buttocks, massaging them as he took him deeper. Clive all but collapsed on top of him.

When it was all said and done, he turned and looked at Trevor. "You know I'm not going to be worth a damn now."

"I believe I was promised food."

"It was only a strong suggestion. Not a promise." Clive covered his eyes with his arm. "You've destroyed me here. I don't think my legs are going to be able to carry me to the elevator, let alone into the village."

"We can always call room service. As a matter of fact, let's do that, and we can sit in bed and eat."

Clive got a devilish look in his eyes. "Make sure you get something that's hard to lick off."

"One order of maple syrup coming up."

Clive smiled and lay back down.

Trevor didn't plan to do anything more the rest of the night but eat and make love to Clive. Now he'd been with him, he wanted to spend as much time in bed as he could before he left. And why not? If Clive was willing, Trevor was more than able. He had to admit, it felt really good to be so carefree and open with someone.

It was better than anything medicine could design.

Chapter Thirteen

THE WATER was beautiful, crystalline and sparkling like jewels. The skies above were a shade of blue Trevor didn't remember ever seeing before—it was different somehow. Bluer.

A smile touched his lips. He couldn't help it. No matter how trite or clichéd it sounded, it really was the beginning of a new life for him. A turning point. From here on out, he'd be able to face life and live it like he gave a shit. The empty feeling in his gut he'd thought would never be filled wasn't even a dull ache now.

Trevor didn't know what tomorrow might bring, but for once he wasn't worried about it either—he was just going to concentrate on enjoying the here and now.

Marlie took a place next to him, holding a bottle of water out for him. "Here. You look thirsty."

Trevor gave a surprised laugh. "I do?"

"Well, maybe not, but it was a good opening line. Don't you think?" She wrinkled her nose, causing her sunglasses to ride up a bit.

"A classic. Can't go wrong with it. But I have to knock off points for lacking originality." He took the water and cracked the seal on it.

"You know I couldn't help but notice Clive is in a very good mood today."

Trevor smiled and turned away. His gaze slammed right into Clive's. The sexy bastard gave him a heated look before turning away to inspect a tank. "He lives a life most people would envy. Why shouldn't he be in a good mood?"

Marlie knocked against Trevor's shoulder. "He is in an *exceptionally* good mood."

Trevor turned to Marlie, trying to look the innocent. "And what makes you think it has anything to do with me?"

"He's got a hickey on the back of his neck."

Heat suffused Trevor's face with the speed of a nuclear strike. "Should we tell him?"

Marlie shook her head. "No. Let him wonder why everyone is snickering behind his back."

Trevor laughed. "Oh, that's so wrong."

"Yeah, but if the tables were turned he'd do the same. Besides, Clive is so not one to talk about that side of his personal life. He is ultimately a gentleman in gigolo's clothing." She gazed over to where Clive still worked. "Well, maybe not at the moment."

Trevor considered Clive's outfit: a pair of shorts and a shirt. There was nothing outstanding or even out of the ordinary about it. Trevor should know; the clothes were his. They'd woken up too late for Clive to run back to his house to change, so he'd borrowed some of Trevor's clothes. The outfit Trevor had of Clive's was still at the hotel laundry.

Trevor lifted his legs, resting his arms on his knees. "He looks good."

"Yeah, I don't think I've ever seen him wear that outfit before." Marlie's eyes were barely visible behind the sunglasses. She cut a look Trevor's way, and he caught the flash of bright blue around the corner of the frames.

Trevor shrugged. "If Clive doesn't talk, don't expect to get anything from me. I'll respect his privacy."

The boat bobbed in the water. It was a perfect day for a dive. Seas were gentle and had only the occasional wave breaking the surface calm.

Carlos drove the boat around the end of the jetties and rounded the island, going parallel to the shoreline. The sheer cliff rose high and steep.

"Where are the caves we're diving?"

"You can't see them from here." Marlie pointed to the cliff face. "They're completely submerged, even during low tide."

"So we're really cave diving, not simply diving inside caves." Clarification was needed before he decided if he was going to punk out and stay on the boat or go into the water with the rest of them.

"Oh, no. The only access is underwater. Once you get inside, there is a cavern that opens up. You can take off your regulator and walk around. It's pretty cool."

"I'll take your word for it."

Marlie grabbed his arm and started pumping it up and down. "Oh, come on. You're going to go, right? Clive's going to want to show you the caves. He loves it there."

"Marlie!" Clive called. "Quit manhandling the guy, will you?"

"He's going to chicken out and not dive with us."

Clive canted his head. "Really?"

Disappointment hit Trevor as surely as if Clive had thrown it at him in the form of a baseball. "I never said that. I only asked if the caves were completely underwater. That's all."

Clive put down the regulator he was holding and came over to where Trevor sat. "Does that bother you?"

"I've never dived like that before. I'm just not sure how well I'm going to do knowing I'll be boxed in for a while." Just thinking about it made him feel as if he was running out of air.

Clive's brow furrowed into a look of concern. He took a seat next to Trevor. "Are you claustrophobic?"

"Not that I've ever noticed. I don't freak out in elevators or going through the tunnels into New York. Small spaces don't make me cringe." He tried to think back to any time in his life that he'd felt he needed to get out of a tight place or pass out, and there wasn't one. "I'm going to say no."

Clive patted Trevor's knee. The touch sent a sensual thrill racing through Trevor's body. "If you don't want to go, that's cool. I don't want you to do something that's going to make you uncomfortable."

"I said I'm good. I'll make it happen."

"I don't want you to panic down there and start using up all your air." As if needing to touch Trevor was a vital part of life at the moment, Clive rubbed a gentle hand over Trevor's neck.

Comfort and affection bloomed, making Trevor's chest feel tight. "It was a one-off comment that's been taken too seriously."

"When it comes to safety of the divers on my watch, there isn't any such thing as 'too seriously.'"

"I know." Trevor's gaze fastened to Clive's sensuous mouth. "And if I didn't think I could handle this, I'd admit it. I'm not trying to be a hero here."

"All right." Clive tightened his grip. "Let me know if you start feeling panicky, and I'll bring you back to the surface. Okay?"

"Deal."

"Generally I certify people before allowing them to dive a cave, but this one is straight forward and well marked. You won't get lost or turned around. And you'll be with me."

Trevor gave a nod. "I trust you."

Clive gave him one last squeeze, then went back to his checks, leaving Trevor with Marlie.

When Clive had his back to them, Trevor shook his head. "That'll teach me."

"Oh, come on. It was for your own good."

"And what good would that be? To make him worry about me once we're down there? He doesn't need to babysit me." Trevor glanced out at the ocean.

Marlie leaned closer, lowering her voice. "He cares about you."

"He cares about everyone on his boat. It's his job."

Trevor only pointed out the obvious to deflect the other divers' attention from his and Clive's budding romance. People were turning and starting to stare. Their ears bent, trying to take in the conversation.

All of them were close friends with Clive and no doubt knew him a hell of a lot better than Trevor did in the short days of their acquaintance—though he doubted any of them had slept with Clive. He seemed pretty determined to keep his love life and friendships in separate compartments. The fact Trevor had been invited along with the others was probably a major step forward for Clive.

Juan Pablo pulled the boat close to the cliffs.

"Let's suit up," Clive called to the group at large.

Trevor waited and let the others go ahead of him. There was no reason to rush. Plenty of time and room for everyone. He took a deep breath and let it out slowly, trying to calm his racing heart.

Yeah, probably not the best way to go into this particular situation.

"Trev? You coming?" Clive stood at the back of the boat expectantly.

"Let everyone else get going, and I'll bring up the rear with you."

Clive gave him a sexy half smile. "That sounds like a really good idea."

Oh hell. He hadn't meant for it to sound like a double entendre.

Their night together had been the best Trevor had spent in a long time. Feelings like those were bound to make the participants turn into fourteen-year-old boys, snickering at every phrase that even came close to sounding dirty. Not very mature of either of them, but then, at the start of a relationship—and one that had a time limit on it—was that even necessary? Who were they trying to impress by acting all adult? The important thing was to enjoy each other for the temporary limit of Trevor's stay. The rest of the relationship stuff was immaterial.

One by one the divers went over the side, pairing up once they were in the water. Trevor walked to the end of the boat and put on his wetsuit, then donned the tanks, regulator, and mask.

"You ready?" Clive asked before putting the regulator in his mouth.

Trevor nodded. It was now or never. Time to do something he'd never done before. Suddenly the panic eased, and excitement of another kind filled his heart.

When this was over, he could say he had done something new and different. He doubted many people he knew back home could boast that they had spelunked with a hot divemaster.

Trevor gave Clive a thumbs-up and went over the side. He swam out of the way and waited for Clive to jump in.

Sunlight penetrated the water and reflected off the sand, making the area easy to see. Surprisingly the water in this area of the cove wasn't very deep and was clear enough to see the bottom.

The mouth of the cave was ahead maybe fifty feet and went all the way down to the ocean floor. The other divers passed through the opening, getting lost in the dark. Clive swam next to him, taking Trevor's hand, imitating kissing the back of it. Whether for luck or inspiration, Trevor wasn't sure, but took the gesture for what it seemed—a sweet form of encouragement.

As they hit the cave entrance, Clive switched on the dive light, allowing them to see into the gloom ahead of them. Fish and other marine life hid in the protective walls of the cave. Along the way, Clive pointed out places in the rock where primitive carvings were chiseled at a level about chest high on an average-size man. It was an amazing sight that hinted at a history long before Rodrigo and Juanita had ever come to the island's shores.

Other places were names and dates of people who had been to the cave, some of them as early as the 1500s. Trevor pointed to one of the dates and gave Clive a quizzical look.

Clive indicated he'd answer once they reached their destination. This was done with a few simple hand gestures that got the point across. A bit farther down, there was a series of metal rods coming from the wall.

Twenty yards away and they came to the opening Marlie had mentioned. The ground came up to meet them, and it was only a matter of walking up the bank and into the cave proper.

Trevor took out the regulator and unhooked the belt on the tanks so he could turn them off.

The chamber was amazing. Stalactites and stalagmites were peppered throughout the cave like the teeth of a long-dead sea creature. He felt a bit like Jonah sitting in the belly of the whale.

Crystals sparkled off the dive lights and lanterns the other divers had set up around the room. Sound from a hidden waterfall echoed in the distance.

Trevor turned to Clive. "This place is amazing."

Clive gave a heated smile. "I knew you'd like it. I've been here hundreds of times over the years, and I never get tired of it. There's always something new to discover or see."

"The dates on the wall. What were those about?"

"This used to be a popular place for smugglers to hide their stash. Of course I suspect at one time the entrance wasn't covered and they could get at least lifeboats in and out of the entrance." Clive gestured toward the entrance. "I imagine earthquakes and other natural disasters probably obscured the entrance over time."

"How did you find it?"

"It's no great secret on the island. Not among serious divers." Clive gave a shrug and set his light down on a rock. "If you look up, you can see old casks and barrels the smugglers left behind."

Trevor glanced up, and sure enough, on one of the ledges shipping crates and barrels were stacked as if waiting for the smuggler to return for his cache. "I think it's remarkable that no one has tried to take them out of here and see what's inside."

"It's kind of an unspoken agreement that those aren't fair game. They stay here."

Trevor put his hands on his hips. "You're going to tell me there's a smuggler's curse, aren't you?"

Mischief twinkled in the depths of Clive's eyes. "I never said that."

"You didn't have to. I've figured out you're a frustrated storyteller."

Clive gave a self-deprecating shrug. "What can I say? The island is a hotbed of legends."

Trevor watched Clive closely, assessing him and the look on his face. "You really love it here, don't you?"

Clive turned to look at him. "Yes. I do. This place—Santa Juanita—saved my sanity."

"I can see that." Trevor left the conversation there and walked off to explore.

Marlie stood at the opening of another chamber. She crooked her arm for Trevor to join her. He went over to her in his flipper-hindered state. She looked down at his feet.

"Didn't Clive make you bring water shoes to put on?"

"He never mentioned it."

"It's much easier to tuck a pair in your belt or inside your suit and then change once you get into the cave. You don't want to walk around on this floor without footwear. You'll cut your feet all to hell and back." She started through the opening.

"Yeah, thanks for telling me that now." Trevor followed her into the secondary chamber.

This one was much larger than the first. The roar from the waterfall grew in volume and intensity. Marlie flashed the dive light in that direction.

Judging from how high up the waterfall emerged from the cave wall, it had to be fed by an underground water system. "Is that fresh or salt water?"

Marlie gave an incredulous laugh. "I'm not sure. I've never tasted it."

"Just wondered if it was fed from the ocean or the island's fresh water source." He wanted to get closer, but the fins prohibited him from climbing up on the rocks.

Clive came up behind him and hit him on the arm with something rubbery.

Trevor looked down at a pair of water shoes. "Thanks."

"I meant to give them to you earlier."

"You're slipping, man." Trevor took the shoes and changed out of the fins.

Clive placed his hand in Trevor's. "Come on, I want to show you something you might find interesting."

Trevor followed Clive to the back of the chamber and into a small alcove. A miniature shrine was set up, complete with a badly eroded carving of the Virgin Mary with arms outspread as if welcoming the humble and downtrodden into her protections.

"It's said that Gutierrez put that here to honor Juanita."

Along the top of the shrine, carved into the cave wall were the words *Rest in peace, dearest sister* in Spanish.

"Why would he put them in the cave and how did he get down here?"

"I think at one time there was another entrance from the topside. See here?" Clive shone the light in the corner, where a wall of rocks had filled an opening. There were more chisel marks along the seam, partially hidden. "This chamber was much bigger at one time."

"Amazing." Trevor felt along the edge of the rocks. Air blew across his fingertips from a hidden passage.

"Are you glad you came down here?"

"Very."

THEY GOT back on the boat and went around the next set of jetties to a small cove where they docked and set up a picnic. Clive leaned back on the grass and closed his eyes. As far as days went, this one was about as perfect as it got.

He'd spent the night making love to an incredible man whose smile alone was enough to heat Clive's blood. Then to be able to show him the caves was a bonus he'd never expected when he'd first met Trevor.

So many things had changed from that initial meeting. Had it really only been about a week? Hard to believe. There were times when he felt he'd known Trevor forever.

Trevor was about as close to Clive's ideal of life partner material as he'd ever knocked up against. Too bad he was only a temporary guy.

Dangerous thoughts crept into Clive's mind. He'd promised himself if he went down this road he wasn't going to wish for more than Trevor could give. Yeah, easier promised than done now that he knew Trevor's touch, kiss, and body intimately.

His friends talked quietly and laughed over jokes told in several languages. He felt someone sit down next to him and looked over.

Trevor plopped onto the blanket, looking out over the water. The sun had slipped down past the midday sky and started on its journey toward the horizon. Only a few puffy white clouds spoiled the otherwise pristine view.

"How much longer do you have on your vacation?"

"Two weeks, then I head back home." Trevor glanced over. "Would I sound crazy if I said I could care less about going back?"

"If you were anyone else, probably not. But knowing how you live for your work…." Clive let the words trail off and sat up. His heart was in his throat. "Are you thinking about staying?"

He watched Trevor swallow, then turn away.

"No. Not as such."

Disappointment was a terrible taste in his mouth. "Then what?"

"Maybe I'll tender my resignation." Trevor's hands rested between his bent knees. They were relaxed. "I should probably look for another job first. Can't afford to be out of work after this vacation."

"Oh, you mean your boss didn't pay for it after he exiled you?" Clive teased.

"Airfare, ride to the airport, and got me an excellent package deal on the resort. He's a good guy that way, but I did have to pay for the actual accommodations. Geoffrey wasn't about to go that far." Trevor gave a slight eye roll. "Still, he's not a bad boss overall. He pretty much leaves me alone to do my own thing—except this latest bit."

"The one the phone call was about?"

"Yes." Trevor made a face of distaste. "It's his company. Let him do what he wants and when it bites him in the ass, he'll know I was right."

"And your coworkers?"

"Believe me, this will dent the company, but it won't put it under." Trevor leaned back on his elbows. "I can see a lot of bonuses going the way of the dodo, though."

Clive rolled to his side and looked at Trevor. "People tend to count on their bonuses if they're used to getting them every year."

"That's the thing, isn't it? They are bonuses. They're never guaranteed in the first place."

Trevor had a point there. It was Clive's bonus checks, horded like a squirrel with a cache of nuts in a tree, that had afforded him the ability to move down to the island. If not for that money, he'd have been stuck in the States, too close to his family for comfort.

"Come on, guys. We're going to set up for volleyball," Marlie called. "We need your spikability, Clive."

Trevor gave a groan. "I suck at volleyball."

"Then stick with me. I'll make you look good."

Chapter Fourteen

THE BOAT came into the dock as the sun sank heavy in the sky. Orange, purple, and gold filled the horizon in wide ribbons of color. Clouds reflected the light, turning them peach and lavender. It was a sight Trevor could never tire of seeing. New Jersey weather tended to be unpredictable at the best of times, brutal at the worst.

All equipment had been cleaned and stored on the way into dock. Clive helped to secure the boat, then let all his friends off. He looked relaxed and happy. Trevor took a deep breath and let it out slowly. He'd like to think that maybe in some small way he'd been responsible for putting that contented look on his lover's face—even if only for a moment.

Juan Pablo, Carlos, and the rest of the gang said good-bye and stood on the dock talking, making plans for when they all showered and changed. From where Trevor stood, it sounded as if they were leaning toward going to the resort pool bar and hanging out over dinner. Marlie walked on the other side of Clive, trying to persuade him to join whatever plans they decided on.

For his part, Trevor just wanted to be alone with Clive for a while, enjoy his company, and maybe Rodger's. The thought of the parrot put a smile on his face. That damn bird was hard to resist.

Clive headed up the dock. Trevor walked a few steps behind him. A man pushed his way through the knot of Clive's friends, head down.

A flash of fading sunlight on metal, a bump, and Clive looked down at his side. He held his hand as blood ran through his fingers. Surprised eyes shot to Trevor's before sliding away.

Clive turned to Marlie. "Don't let Trevor see this."

It was too damn late. Trevor had already witnessed the entire incident.

A sick feeling bloomed from somewhere deep in Trevor's soul. Flashes from Jason's death lit up like a movie reel moving in slow motion through his mind.

This was not happening again. It wasn't!

Trevor froze for a moment before he snapped back into real time. The culprit took off running down the dock, away from the resort.

"Stop him! He stabbed Clive!" Trevor pointed in the direction of the suspect.

He'd only seen the man's face briefly, but it was enough to identify him as the one from the festival, though this time his face was filled with anger and determination instead of red paint.

Juan Pablo took off at a run. Carlos jumped the fence and headed up the hill to intercept.

"I can't breathe," Clive muttered between bloodstained lips.

"I know." A well of calm opened inside Trevor. Where it came from he hadn't a clue, but he used it to fuel him. "He's punctured your lung. I'm going to lay you down now. I need to take a look at the injury."

Clive gripped Trevor's hand with white knuckles.

Trevor glanced up at Clive's friend. "Marlie, I need you to do a few things for me, and I need you to do them quickly. First, I need medical transport to a center that can handle a punctured lung. Secondly, I need scissors and heavy-duty tape."

She stood there nodding but didn't move.

"Now, Marlie! Move!"

She came back to herself and started to pull her phone from her pocket as she took off for the kiosk.

"There... is... a... med... ic... al...."

"Shut up, Clive. Do not talk. Concentrate on breathing. I'm going to do what I can for you here, but I might have to waste your wetsuit."

Clive managed to lift his hand. He wasn't looking good. Blood probably pooled in the pleural space. He needed intubated, but Trevor doubted there was anything like intubation equipment at the resort. Hadn't Clive mentioned they were looking for a qualified doctor? Shit, there was no way he could handle this injury with what Clive carried in his rucksack.

Marlie returned with her phone still tucked to her ear. She was speaking in rapid-fire Spanish. Tears streamed down her cheeks. She handed over the scissors and tape with shaking hands.

Clive's breaths came in short, quick pants. Things were deteriorating rapidly.

"How's that transport coming?"

"On their way." Marlie knelt down beside Trevor. "What can I do to help?"

"Who are you talking to?"

"Medics from the clinic."

"Ask if they have intubation equipment, oxygen tanks, and an Ambu bag."

She used a mix of Spanish and English to get the point across. "They said yes. They'll be here in a few minutes."

"Good. Now hang up and go through Clive's rucksack and grab anything you can find that's made from a thin sheet of plastic. Rubber gloves, anything."

She did so, rummaging in the bag as shouts filled the parking lot the next level above their heads. Marlie pulled out a square bag filled with what looked like vitamins. "Will this work?"

"Perfect. Lay it across the palm of your hand and hold your hand over the wound while I work on making a dressing."

"The sun is almost down."

Trevor had noticed that but tried to ignore it. "Do these lights along the docks come on automatically?"

Marlie nodded and sniffled. "Yes."

"Then I'm not going to worry about it at the moment." Though it would have been nice to see Clive's color. Trevor tried not to think about it—he could only do one thing at a time, and Marlie had her hands full. If Clive stopped breathing they were going to need another set of hands and lungs pronto.

Trevor cut a piece of the neoprene wetsuit and set it on top of the plastic Marlie held. Then he taped the makeshift bandage in place on three sides.

"That's as good as I can do for now." Trevor moved to Clive's face and touched his forehead. "Hang in there. We're getting you transferred to someplace where they can take care of you."

Clive reached out for Trevor's hand and gripped it in the darkness.

Nausea turned Trevor's stomach. This was not happening. Not again. The words *don't you dare die on me* were on the tip of his tongue, but he bit them back with a force he didn't know he possessed.

Trevor didn't want Clive to know exactly how serious the situation was. Shouts exploded down the dock along with the sound of running feet. Trevor looked up and saw medics coming with a stretcher in tow.

"They're here, Clive. Hang in there."

The medics swarmed. They started asking questions, but all of Trevor's rudimentary Spanish failed him. Marlie translated, giving them the picture of what had transpired and what Trevor had managed to do to help.

At least that's what he supposed. He'd shut down to only the small plane of existence where his and Clive's hands connected.

One of the medics crawled up to Clive's head and straightened his neck. Trevor closed his eyes. They were going to intubate Clive before transport to the medical facility. Good. It was harder to do such an invasive procedure in route. Still, he found it difficult to watch—no matter how many times he'd witnessed and performed them himself.

The medic was good—Trevor would give him that. The tube went in on the first shot. Blood came up the endotracheal tube from the injury. Not unexpected, but it made Trevor run cold.

The medics got Clive on the stretcher and started away with him. Trevor and Marlie followed behind.

"Where are they taking him?"

"There's a hospital on the other side of the island."

"Can they handle this?"

"Probably not, but they have a landing place and air transport over to the mainland." Marlie squeezed his hand. "They'll be able to stabilize him there. It's better than what we have on this side."

"How do I get there?" There was no way in hell Trevor was going to stay behind at the resort and wait for word.

"We'll have to go over by boat. There's no way they're going to let you ride in the helicopter with them."

No, he didn't suppose they would.

"All right. When is the last ferry to the mainland?"

Marlie glanced at her phone. "If we hurry, we can just make it."

"Wait. We need someone to take care of Rodger."

"Don't worry. I'll call Juan Pablo. He might have a key to Clive's place."

Now that the initial adrenaline rush had passed, Trevor's legs shook and his stomach roiled. He wasn't long for staying on his feet. He kept moving forward, hoping the underside didn't hit him before he made it to the ferry.

Lights from police vehicles in the parking lot flashed, filling the night with neon blue. Trevor glanced over in time to see one of the police shove someone into the back of an SUV. Juan Pablo and Carlos were talking to two of the other officers.

Marlie pointed to the knot of people. "I think they caught him."

"Looks like it." Anger flooded Trevor's veins. He made a beeline for the SUV. The bastard had hunted Clive down for days—Trevor had no doubt in his mind the intention had always been to harm him. But for what reason? Because Clive had embarrassed the asshole at a friendly festival? How demented did someone have to be to see that as a reason to try and kill a guy?

Trevor came up on the other side of the truck, facing away from the cops. Just one good punch, that's all he wanted. A chance to just knock the fucker the fuck out.

Marlie grabbed Trevor's arm and tried to restrain him from grabbing the door handle. "Don't. If you do this, the police will detain you and you'll never make that ferry to the mainland tonight."

It was a point worth considering, but in no way did it make him feel better.

Marlie yelled over to Juan Pablo about Rodger. He turned from the police and gave a nod.

"Come on, Trevor. We have to hurry."

As if hearing her urgency, the ferry's whistle blew.

"That's the first one. We have five minutes left to get there. How good a sprinter are you?"

"Fair to middling, but with this bum knee I'm not going to be able to go very fast."

"Just go as fast as you can." Marlie grabbed his arm and started dragging him behind her. The woman was surprisingly strong for her size.

He hadn't brought his cane today. Didn't think he'd need it. The motions used for swimming seemed to soothe his knee. This running—not good.

His knee tried to twist again, but he held the joint locked in place, and ran in a bastardization of a three-legged race and Frankenstein's monster. It wasn't the best choice, but at least he was on his way to a hospital. If he injured it too badly trying to make the ferry, he'd have them take an X-ray once he arrived.

Each beat of his heart brought fresh pain shooting through his leg. Anger seethed in his veins, a rolling boil that preceded the blowing of a volcano.

Who was that guy and why did he stab Clive? What could have set him off enough to arouse that level of violence? Not to mention, if Clive had been alone, would the assailant have kept stabbing him until he died? The thought chilled. Had he been a disgruntled ex-lover, a rival, or had winning against him in the wrestling match been enough to make him wig out?

They finally made it to the dock. The boat was getting ready to leave. Marlie shoved a coin into the slot of the turnstile, then pushed through.

With a sinking feeling, Trevor felt his pockets. "I don't have any coins."

Marlie doubled back, turning to the boat. She yelled something at one of the operators. When he shook his head and shrugged, she went at him with anger.

Spanish had always sounded like a passionate language to Trevor, but even more so now when his lover's friend went to bat for him.

Tired of the argument and not getting anywhere, Trevor slid under the turnstile and threw paper money at the man. "Here's your lousy fare, now get moving."

Trevor didn't know if it was the angry English, the overpayment to get on the boat, or the fact his expression probably conveyed just how bad a mood he was in, but the man picked up the cash and stuffed it into his pocket, then gave the signal to the captain to pull away from the dock.

Marlie shot the ferry attendant a nasty look but smiled at Trevor. "Nice move."

"Thanks. It's called throwing money at the problem."

The boat started a slow chug through the channel and out to the open sea. The vessel was bigger than the ferries Trevor used to cross the Hudson. This one had two decks for cars and one for pedestrians. The railings and outdoor seating were also people-friendly—the crew was not.

Trevor glanced down and noticed his hands and shirt were covered in blood. That probably explained the operator's reaction more than anything else. Letting a guy bathed in blood onto the boat was not going to be a happy proposition for those ensuring the safety of the other passengers.

He took a seat and stared out at the last dregs of sunshine as they disappeared on the horizon. History had a horrible way of repeating itself. It was like some stupid cosmic joke had just taken a shit on his head.

He felt Marlie's steady gaze on him but didn't look at her. He didn't want to talk at the moment. Just wanted to sit quietly and think about what he'd done in this life to be dumped on twice by the universe. Wasn't he supposed to be happy? Was that it? Fine. If it meant Clive got to live, he'd give up any feelings he had for the guy and walk away. It was a small price to pay to ensure a life was spared.

Trevor rested his arm up on the railing, then laid his head down.

It had been a perfect day. One of the most magical and fun he'd had in a very long time. So long he didn't even remember the last time. To taint it in violence was unfair.

And Clive. He didn't deserve this. Not even the first bit.

Trevor closed his eyes and hoped for a short ride.

Chapter Fifteen

TREVOR WOKE to a soft shake of his shoulder. His eyes were crusty and dry, either from the salt air or fatigue, he wasn't sure.

"We're here." Marlie stood and smoothed out her rumpled T-shirt. For the first time, Trevor noticed she was in as bad shape as he. Blood covered her palms and the backs of her fingers. There was a rusty-brown handprint across the bottom of her shirt where she'd placed her hand after holding the makeshift dressing on Clive's side.

"Maybe we should find a bathroom in the ferry station and clean up a bit before we get to the hospital." His suggestion met with a shake of her head.

"We'll need to hurry if we're going to grab a taxi before the others do."

"What happens if we don't?"

"We'll be forced to wait until they circle back around after dropping off their passengers. It could take a while."

Things were just not the same as at home. He was used to the airports, ports, and bus stations in and around the New York/New Jersey area. Taxis were plentiful, and if one wasn't available, it only took a few minutes to find one.

Trevor made a face. "That's just wrong on so many levels."

"Come on. This is going to be kind of a race." Marlie didn't seem too thrilled with the prospect.

Trevor stood and followed her to the disembarking platform. "Should I be worried about that?"

"Depends on how your leg is and if you mind knocking people out of the way."

"Oh, so it's pretty much like grabbing a cab in New York." Truthfully he'd never had a hard time getting a cab in the city.

Marlie turned back to glance at him. "I wouldn't know. I've never been there. I grew up in San Diego."

Trevor had nothing to say to that—only small talk, and this clearly wasn't the time or place. Besides he was concentrating too hard on trying to get his legs to work without shaking. Each step he took required concentration to get his foot to land how he wanted and to keep his knees from buckling. He doubted Marlie would appreciate him going out on her on the way to find a taxi.

They came off the concourse and through a small terminal to the front of the station. The building reminded him faintly of the Port Imperial in Weehawken, with the exception of colorful murals on the walls instead of drab gray-blue paint.

They stepped out into the humid night air. Marlie grabbed his hand and ran for a taxi at the very end of the line. It made sense. Most people were swarming around the vehicles near the door, waving money as if they were about to haggle on the price.

They slid into the back of the cab.

Marlie leaned forward. *"Leve-nos o hospital. Depresso!"*

The driver hit the gas, and they pulled away from the curb with all the grace of an Indy car at the 500. They weaved in and out of the heavy city traffic. Trevor remembered this view as he'd prepared to go to the resort. It was much different in the back of a speeding cab at night.

They pulled up to the emergency entrance as a helicopter flew in low and landed on a special pad away from the hospital proper.

Marlie hit Trevor's arm. "That's probably Clive. Good timing."

It was miraculous timing as far as he was concerned. He'd felt as if they were on that damn ferry for hours. Staff from the ER ran out to the helipad, bending low to keep out of the range of the blades. They brought the stretcher out, and the team ran with them into the ER.

Trevor didn't get a good look at the patient as they rolled by. Too many people were around the stretcher. "Come on, let's go to the desk and ask if he's gotten here yet."

Marlie led him into the ER through the main entrance and around the counter to the reception area. At first glance, Trevor was impressed by the modern, clean, and professional atmosphere of the hospital. Not that he should be—Brazil was a very modern country. Granted there were some parts that were covered in rainforest and lacked civilization, but hell, that was true of many parts of the US as well.

Marlie conversed with the receptionist for a moment. There were a few head nods and questions asked and answered. She gave what was clearly a *thank you* and walked away. Lost, Trevor followed Marlie like a trained retriever to the waiting room.

They sat down. People turned to stare at their blood-covered clothes.

"What did the receptionist say?"

"That was him we saw coming in. It's going to be a while before anyone comes out to talk to us." She leaned closer and lowered her voice. "And if anyone asks, you're his brother visiting from the States. It's the only way they're going to let you or me in to see him later."

"Got it." But it stung. He wasn't really anything—a lover, but that was only a temporary position at best. There really wasn't a category he fit into at the moment. He wasn't even a potential significant other. Did Brazil acknowledge those associations? He hadn't considered it when he'd decided to come to South America and the islands off Brazil's shores. It hadn't seemed important at the time.

Trevor linked his blood-stained hands together and lowered his head to rest on them. It was going to be a long wait. If they hadn't placed a chest tube in Clive at the hospital on Santa Juanita, then that was the first priority. Trevor shuddered to think they'd let Clive go that long without one.

Had he done the right thing? Were his efforts all in vain? No. He wasn't going to think like that—not going to second-guess himself. Clive had been alive when Trevor handed off his care to the medics. If anything, he'd given Clive the chance to make it to this stage of care.

Nervous energy vibrated through Trevor. He shot to his feet and limped around the waiting room, trying to work some of it off. He was on his second circuit around when he noticed the public restrooms tucked over in a corner.

He ducked into the men's room and straight to the sinks. Blood crusted his hands, front and back. It had gotten under his nails and stuck there.

He turned on the tap and shoved his hands under, rubbing them in a way that would make Lady Macbeth proud. The soap dispenser was full, but a steady drip had made a foamy mound underneath. He hit the lever and nothing happened. When he pulled his hand back, the soap made a slow drip from the nozzle.

"Really?"

He curled his hand into a fist, ready to punch the fucking thing, but the door opened and someone else entered.

What in the hell was he doing? Going to take his frustrations out on an inanimate object? Oh, yeah, that was grown up.

He pressed the lever again and waited. The soap came out in a liquid ooze no bigger than a dime into his palm. It wasn't a lot, but it would at least get the job started. Now that he knew the trick to the dispenser, he could get more if needed. What he really wanted was a scrub brush.

He stood at the sink washing his hands for a few minutes before the door opened again and Marlie stuck her head in.

"Christ, Marlie, this is the men's room!"

"Come on, it's not like it's the first time I've ever seen one." She frowned. "I was worried about you."

"I'm fine. Washing my hands. I'll be out in a few."

She retreated, and the door closed behind her with a quiet click.

Trevor finished in the restroom and exited. The waiting room had emptied some since he'd gone inside. Thank goodness. He really didn't want a lot of noise or conversations going on around him. He just wanted to huddle in a corner somewhere and wait in silence.

Even if he hadn't practiced medicine in years, he wished he was allowed into the trauma room. At least he'd be able to see what was going on instead of this horrible waiting for word. He sat on a hard plastic chair and curled into the wall, trying to shut out the others in the room as well as the past. Images from that night eight years ago kept trying to leak over onto the present.

His gut churned and his heart ached.

Echoes of the last moments in the ER in New York trailed through his mind in a constant loop.

"I'm sorry. Mr. Donner was dead on arrival. There was nothing we could do for him."

Trevor sat there for another thirty minutes, unmoving, unable to process. They had asked him if he wanted to see Jason one last time. He had, but the ability to physically pick himself up from the chair and walk into the room had been more than he could bear.

In the end it was his mother who had gone in with him to see Jason. Everything that had made Jason special no longer existed. All the animation and life had drained from his face, leaving him looking no better than a wax model from a movie set.

It wasn't *his* Jason.

Trevor turned in his chair and looked at Marlie. "I think I'm going to go out of my fucking mind if I sit here any longer."

She gave him a look of sympathy. "I know. Clive was the first friend I made when I moved to Santa Juanita. As a matter of fact, he's the one who got me the job at the resort. He's probably the closest thing to family I have in the world and…." Her stoic demeanor broke. Her pretty face crumbled into tears. "If I lose him, I don't know what I'll do."

Shame filled Trevor's cheeks with heat. He'd been conceited, stupid, and self-involved, not once worrying about what Clive's true friends were suffering.

Trevor took her hand in his and squeezed. "He'll pull through. He's a strong guy. And loves life too much to give it up."

So had Jason, but Trevor refrained from saying so—there was no need to resurrect his tragic love life at a time like this. Not when it made him look like a romantic jinx.

"Have you ever read the report? Maybe you should."

Clive's words came back to him. Clarity dawned, and he reached for his phone, then stopped. It was really late in New Jersey. His parents would have gone to bed long ago. A late-night phone call about something that had waited eight years would only make them worry. He'd call his mother in the morning.

Until then, he had to hang on and hope his prayers were answered.

Chapter Sixteen

PAIN WAS an unbearable bitch of an enemy. It bit into his side without mercy or care. Relief was a light in the distance, small at first but growing with every breath Clive took. For the most part, he was in and out of consciousness. His entire existence had narrowed down to the flashes of intense agony in his side and the microscopic pull of air through the straw in his throat.

They hadn't given him enough for pain or sedation. Each time the medication wore off, fresh agony ripped through him.

Every time he tried to signal them to help him, someone held his hand down and refused to listen. Frustration put him at the breaking point.

Where was Trevor?

Had he been hurt too?

Blackness came quickly and without warning.

Sounds faded in and out, radio stations with poor reception. Everyone spoke a mix of Spanish and Portuguese. He had a hard time deciphering what they wanted, when they asked him anything at all. Mostly they poked and prodded and caused more pain.

Another knife. This one brought his back off the bed as someone stuffed something big and round between his ribs. His eyes flew open to bright lights and shouts. There was a horrible sucking sound, then air—blessed, life-saving air.

He slept.

The next time he woke, it was to a man standing over him speaking in Portuguese. He must have gotten onto the mainland somehow. Clive raised his hand to indicate he didn't understand. The man—doctor—patted his hand to reassure, then simulated coughing.

Did he want Clive to cough?

Clive did, and the man pulled out the tube in Clive's throat. He coughed hard. Pain sliced through his side again. He winced. Oh God. He hurt all over. His throat was as raw as if he'd been swallowing sandpaper. His side felt as if the T-Rex from *Jurassic Park* had torn a hole through his midsection. All he really wanted was to know if Trevor was all right.

Christ, he vaguely remembered Trevor bent down over him assessing the wound and holding pressure on it. Did Trevor even know he was still alive?

The doctor walked off, and Clive heard the door open again, though he couldn't see it from the bed because of the closed curtain. He was too sore to move much, and he couldn't reach the curtain even if he could lean over.

There was a distinct sound of metal hooks moving on rails. Footsteps tapped closer to the bed.

"How are you feeling?"

Relief washed through Clive, and he turned toward the voice. He started to speak, but the words came out low and garbled. He cleared his throat. "Like I've been keelhauled. How are you?"

"Better now I can see you're talking and making jokes." Trevor pulled up a chair by the bed. Blood splattered the front of his shirt in dirty-brown stains.

Clive pointed out the spots. "That mine?"

"Yep."

"Glad to hear it. I was afraid he'd gotten you too."

"You should have been more afraid for him. If not for Marlie, I would have pulled him out of the police car and dragged the pavement with him." Trevor frowned. "Why was he after you?"

"I don't even know who he was."

"Same guy who attacked you at the festival."

Clive gave a nod. He was afraid of that, but had no answer to give Trevor. Not at the moment. He needed to talk to the man and find out what his beef was, if he'd even talk. "I don't think he likes me."

"That's an understatement." Trevor stared off, his expression bleak. "By rights I should beat the ever-loving shit out of you for scaring me like that."

Now that warmed Clive's heart like nothing else had that day. Day? Was it still the same day? How long had he been in the hospital? "Sorry. I didn't intend to end the trip with a dockside stabbing."

"No. Neither did I."

"So you patched me up?"

"As much as I could using a plastic bag, electrical tape, and piece of neoprene. I owe you a wetsuit by the way."

Clive started to laugh, but it turned into a cough when the pain struck. "I don't think they believe in pain meds here."

"You hurt?"

"I'm about out of my head with it." He closed his eyes and breathed in and out through his nose to try and work his way around the pain. "I mean, I'm a man and all, but this is even too much for me."

Trevor started to get up. "I'll see what I can do."

Clive held out his hand. "Don't go."

"I just want to find out if you can have something to take the edge off. There's no reason for you to suffer."

"I know, but it's fine at the moment." It was a colossal lie, but Clive really didn't want Trevor to leave him. "I wanted to talk to you."

Trevor swallowed and sat back down. "About what?"

"I know it couldn't have been easy doing what you did, thinking I was going to die on you too. For a few moments there, I thought maybe I was, but you did it. You saved my life." Clive held out his hand, which Trevor took in a shaky yet firm grip. "Thank you."

A suspicious sheen of tears shone in Trevor's eyes before he blinked and glanced down at their entwined hands. "I didn't think I could do it, but I was determined to pull you through."

"If you hadn't been there, I would have died."

Trevor shook his head. "Don't think like that."

"It's true." Clive squeezed Trevor's hand again, loving the way their fingers and palms fit together so naturally. "You leave your mark on people, and you don't even realize it."

Trevor gave a huff that was probably an aborted laugh. "I wasn't the one who stabbed you. I only stuck tape on your chest hair."

"Still, it was something."

"Yes."

They lapsed into silence. Trevor didn't let go of Clive's hand, and truth be told, Clive didn't want him to. His touch was both comfort and companionship. Words seemed so inadequate to express the emotions bubbling to the surface.

How did one properly thank the man who had been instrumental in saving his life when the man didn't want thanks? Maybe it was humility that made Trevor shy away from praise, but that only made him more attractive to Clive. Trevor was a beautiful person inside and out.

Clive raised a brow and glanced at the curtain. "Come closer."

"Why?"

"Just do it."

Trevor leaned closer to the edge of the bed.

"No. Stand up and come here."

Trevor did and bent over the side rail.

"Kiss me."

"I'm supposed to be your brother."

"I could never have brotherly feelings for you, Trev. You're already so much more."

Trevor's face sort of crumbled, then. His mouth turned down at the corners. His eyes slid shut, and he pressed his mouth to Clive's. The kiss was soft, yet passionate, and conveyed feelings neither of them had dared bring up.

When he moved away, Trevor ran his hand down the side of Clive's face. "Did that hurt?"

"No. It felt good. Better than all the pain meds on the mainland."

Trevor ran a thumb teasingly over Clive's bottom lip. "Never underestimate the healing powers of a kiss."

Especially ones given by men who looked like they'd stepped out of a lurid fantasy.

A thought struck him then. He grabbed Trevor's hand. "Rodger."

"Is being taken care of by Juan Pablo."

Clive eased back against the pillows and closed his eyes. That second or two of panic for his best little buddy had taken a lot out of him. "Good. Rodger likes Juan Pablo."

"Rodger was my second thought after getting you into the hands of the medics."

Clive thought he might have smiled, but right about then a nice warm lethargy stole over him, and he went down into the most peaceful slumber he'd had since before getting stabbed.

TREVOR WAITED until Clive fell back to sleep before he sneaked from the room. Now that it was clear Clive was on the road to recovery, it was time to head back to Santa Juanita and take a long overdue shower. A change of clothes was probably a good idea too. He'd check in on Rodger and take him out onto the bluff to stretch his wings and feel the breeze through his feathers.

Marlie traveled with him back to the island. Her usual upbeat and cheery disposition had deteriorated with lack of sleep and coffee. She claimed the vending machine version was only slightly tinted water with a burnt bean taste. Trevor had taken her word for it and steered clear.

Now he was thirsty, hungry, dirty, and tired to the bone.

The sun was going down again. It had been almost forty-eight hours since the stabbing, and he'd never been so glad to see how fast medicine moved at the medical center. Normally someone with the type of chest wound Clive endured would stay intubated for several days.

But the chest tubes had seen his lung inflate and normal breathing return. It could also be a testament to Clive's will to live and heal. A lot could be said for mind over matter.

They reached the docks and a small party waiting for them. Juan Pablo was there with Rodger on his shoulder. The parrot had a little bandana around his neck. When he spotted Trevor, he bounced up and down excitedly.

"*Hot stuff!*"

Trevor found a smile and reached up to take Rodger from Juan Pablo's shoulder. "How's he been?"

"Not himself. I think he knows Clive's not here."

Trevor reached up and stroked Rodger's belly. "Is that right. You miss your best bud?"

Rodger began to pick at Trevor's hair.

"Is Clive going to be all right?" Juan Pablo fell into step beside Trevor as they walked up the dock to the ferry station proper.

"He was sleeping when I left. I just came back to shower, change, and grab something to eat before I head back over to the hospital. Can you watch Rodger for a little longer?"

"*Sí.*"

Marlie and Carlos walked behind them talking quietly. Trevor didn't have the strength or interest to try to eavesdrop on their conversation. He heard Clive's name and some Spanish words, then lost interest. She was probably updating him on their friend's progress.

He walked through the hotel and rode the elevator up to his room, numb from the events of the past day. The adrenaline and fear had subsided, and now the only thing left was a deep well of *been there, done that* threatening to suck him down into oblivion.

He kept having to remind himself that Clive was alive and doing well. However, the side of his brain that knew medicine also worried about pulmonary embolisms and pneumonia. There were still so many things that could go wrong and take Clive away from him.

With his hand on the doorknob, he stopped and placed his head against the door. He'd fallen for Clive. Life without him would not be worth living. Even the thought of going back to the States caused his chest to tighten and air to choke off.

He let himself into the room and set Rodger on the back of his regular chair. A shower might clear his head and help him think properly—and food.

He made a quick order to room service, then jumped in the shower. Water sluiced down his body, taking away grime and sweat. Blood remained under his fingernails, though he'd tried to clean them in the public restroom at the hospital.

He hurried to dress. Room service arrived as he pulled his shirt over his head. The waiter brought the food into the room and set it down on the table in the living room. When he finished, he turned to Trevor.

"How's Clive?"

"Doing better. Thank you for asking."

"Talk is you saved his life."

"I did what I could with what I had." Trevor held his hand out for the bill.

The waiter shook his head. "No. The boss says your stay here is his treat. Anything you want."

Trevor blinked. "I don't know what to say. Tell him thank you, but it's not necessary."

The waiter gave a knowing nod. "He is good friends with Clive. They go diving and fishing together. He would be insulted if you refused."

"Then I humbly thank him for his generosity." Trevor reached into his pocket and pulled out some cash. "Here."

The waiter looked as if he might refuse the money, but one look at Trevor's expression and he nodded in thanks before placing it into his pocket. "Tell Clive that Ernesto and his family pray for him."

"Will do."

After Ernesto left, Trevor took the tray into the bedroom and stretched out with dishes beside him and turned on the television. Local access only had a few English-speaking stations to choose from, but he mostly wanted background noise and nothing he had to necessarily pay attention to.

He turned the volume down and picked up his phone. No return call from his mother. Maybe she hadn't gotten the message he'd left on her voice mail asking her to go to his house and retrieve the manila envelope at the bottom of his desk drawer.

He had no idea why the reason for Jason's death was so important in light of Clive's injury. The outcomes were not the same—but maybe Clive had been right. Trevor had been punishing himself for years over something that might have been out of his control to change.

If so, he'd left a profession he loved for no other reason than fear.

Fear that he couldn't make a difference.

Fear that he might freeze again.

Fear that someone else's loved one might die in his arms.

Trevor ran a hand down his face. During his residency and first few weeks of practice he'd helped more people than he had since. Though that wasn't entirely true, since the medical products Global produced or licensed had helped millions over the years; it was only in a different manner.

He ate his food and drank the bottled water he'd ordered. His eyelids grew too heavy to keep open, so he leaned back against the pillows for a quick snooze.

Sunset loomed beyond the balcony windows when his cell phone rang and woke him. He was groggy and disoriented. It was hard to focus on the phone. The icon was a picture of his mother back in her flower child days.

Seeing her avatar, he came immediately awake.

"I got it. Do you want me to open it?" Her voice was soft, worried sounding.

"Yes. But you don't have to read the entire report to me. Just the conclusion."

"All right."

Trevor glanced around the room. He needed fortification and fast. "Hold on!"

He jumped up and crossed the room to the minibar. There were a couple of bottles of vodka, rum, and gin, along with mixers. No whiskey. Damn.

He made a quick gin and tonic and took a swallow. "All right. I think I'm ready."

"Before I read this to you, can I ask why you're doing this now?"

"It's a good question. A fair one." He rubbed a hand across his gut and tried to stop the churning. "Someone told me I would probably never move on unless I knew the truth, and for once I chose to listen."

"Are you all right other than that?"

Trevor took a deep breath. He'd never lied to his mother—even as a child. She was such a gentle and loving soul he'd never wanted to disappoint or hurt her. "I might have met someone worth leaving Jason's memory behind."

There was a beat of silence. "Oh, honey. I'm so happy for you."

Trevor didn't elaborate; there would be plenty of time to tell both her and his father the entire story when he had more time and rest.

"Cause of death. It says here: deceased died of blood loss resulting from severed aorta due to GSW."

Trevor sat on the bed with his drink hanging limply in his hand. A severed aorta. No wonder there hadn't been time to help Jason.

Relief washed through him. Fast, clean, and overwhelming.

So many years wasted.

He was every bit the fool some had accused him of being, and all because he'd not wanted to know the truth.

"Thank you, Ariel."

"Are you going to be all right? Do you want your father and me to fly down there?"

He laughed through his self-flagellation. "No. I'll be fine. I promise."

"What are you going to do now?"

"First thing—I'm going to quit my job."

Chapter Seventeen

WHEN TREVOR arrived at Clive's room the next morning, Dr. Cheavez was leaving. The doctor greeted him with a nod.

"Excuse me. Can I have a word with you for a moment?"

Cheavez looked down at his watch, then nodded. "Is this about Mr. Ducaine?"

"No, actually, this is about me. I want to know if you can put me in touch with the correct agency to secure my medical license down here. Santa Juanita and the resort in particular are looking for a new physician. It's been a long time since I've practiced, but I have kept up my credentials." Trevor slid his hands down into his pockets to hide the shaking in them. It wasn't like him to ask for help, but he also had no idea how to go about navigating the red tape in a foreign country.

Cheavez smiled and gave Trevor a few taps on the shoulder. "For you, I'd do this without hesitation. You saved your *brother's* life. It is the least I can do for you. The regulating agency is the *Conselho Federal de Medicina.*"

Trevor shook his hand. "Thank you. I'll contact them directly."

"If you should need anything while applying, please do not hesitate to contact me. I will be more than happy to help."

Trevor thanked him again. About the only thing he'd need right off the bat was going to be a refresher course in Spanish and to learn Portuguese from the ground up.

He entered Clive's room. Clive had the television on, flipping through channels, most of which were soap operas with a few news programs thrown in for good measure. He landed on an old Clint Eastwood movie dubbed into Portuguese and left it there, but turned the volume down when he saw Trevor.

"I needed something for background. The quiet is about to drive me batshit crazy."

Trevor took a seat by the bed. "I would have thought you'd appreciate the quiet. Not too noisy up there on your bluff."

"There, I at least have the sound of the ocean and Rodger's constant chatter. Here, nothing." Clive rubbed a hand over his side. The chest tube no longer bubbled.

Trevor stood up and inspected the situation. They'd clamped it off already, which meant Clive's lung was reinflated and they were hoping to pull the catheter out soon. "Nice job. You should be out of here before too long."

"That's what the doctor said. Unfortunately I won't be fit for diving for a while." His mouth turned down at the corners. "Still, it's better than pushing up daisies."

"Any day of the week. May I?" Trevor lifted up Clive's hospital gown and inspected the dressing around the insertion site. A slight redness appeared under the clear borders of the Tegaderm patch, but disappeared under the gauze that covered where the plastic tube entered the skin. There wasn't enough color change to call it an irritation. There was no blood or serous fluid on the dressing. It looked good. Clean. "You're healing nicely."

"Still hurts when I take a deep breath."

Trevor glanced up. "It's going to, especially while you still have the chest tube in."

No doubt it was hard for an active, vital man like Clive to be holed up in bed, flat on his back, waiting until his body healed to do what he wanted. "Is there someone who can take over the duties of divemaster while you fully recover?"

"Juan Pablo can. Phil. There are a few others from the other resort who have filled in for me a time or two. I've already talked to them. It's covered, so my business isn't going to go tits up any time soon."

"That's good to hear."

There was a knock on the door.

"*Entrar!*" Clive called in Portuguese.

Two police officers wearing the uniforms of Santa Juanita came into the room. One was tall and lanky, giving the appearance of youth. The second was short, stocky, and built like a tank. Neither of them wore friendly expressions.

Clive used the remote to turn off the television.

"Señor Ducaine?"

"*Sí.*"

The rest of the conversation was held in rapid-fire Spanish that Trevor had no hope of following. Some of the words he recognized but failed to grasp the context. He imagined they were questioning Clive about the stabbing and the suspect.

When they turned to Trevor to start questioning him, he held up his hand. "In English, please. My Spanish is very poor."

The officers exchanged glances. The shorter of the two took the lead on questioning Trevor.

"You witnessed the stabbing that injured Señor Ducaine?"

"I did." Trevor explained what he'd seen and done in the moments that followed.

The officer, whose badge read Suarez, glanced up from his notebook. "You were the one who saved him?" He indicated Clive lying on the bed by jabbing his pen in Clive's general direction.

"I offered aid until the medics could arrive." It was a particularly slippery slope at the moment. The last thing he needed while contemplating moving to the island and starting a practice out of the resort was to appear to be practicing medicine without a local license. No telling what the rules were in a case like that.

"No, you saved him," Suarez insisted. "It's all over Santa Juanita. He's a very popular man, and we thank you."

Trevor shot a glance over to Clive, who had the audacity to wear an extremely smug expression on his face. "Let me guess. Officer Suarez here is a dive buddy of yours?"

"No, but his brother Ricardo is."

Trevor filed that away for later. "I can identify the suspect. He was the same man who wrestled Clive in the Poco Carlita festival match. Clive beat him, and he attacked him when Clive had his back turned."

Suarez and his partner exchanged looks. "Juan Pablo said he is also the same man who has been searching for you for the past week. Is there bad blood between you?" This was directed at Clive.

Clive shook his head. "I don't know. If there was, it wasn't on my part. I really want a chance to talk to him before you transfer him to the capital jail."

"We can hold him until you are released from here, but no longer I'm afraid." Suarez gave a shrug. "The authorities in Puerto Solis will want to question him."

Puerto Solis was the capital city of Santa Juanita. It was small compared to most capitals Trevor had seen, but then, Santa Juanita was not a very big island.

"*¡Gracias!*" Clive watched them walk out and let out a sigh as he leaned against his pillow. "Oh, no, that wasn't stressful."

"They seemed a bit humorless, but then I didn't catch your conversation with them. Were they accusing you of anything?"

"No. They just wanted to know how well I knew the suspect." Clive's cheeks grew a little pink, and he turned away. "I have a certain reputation on the island."

Trevor's stomach took a sudden dive. Maybe he'd been too hasty thinking he'd chuck it all to try and build a life down here. "And that would be?"

"I like my affairs short and to the point, then move on."

Trevor swallowed down disappointment. "I see."

Clive caught Trevor's gaze and held it. "No. I don't think you do."

Trevor stood. He really didn't need it spelled out any more plainly for him. If Clive wanted to move on, that was fine. The logistics of moving an entire continent away were mind-boggling.

Christ, his heart hurt. It had been a really emotional couple of days, and maybe he needed to go back to the resort, get a good stiff drink, and just sit on the beach and melt into the sand for a while.

Clive leaned over and grabbed Trevor's hand, clasping it tightly. "No. Trust me. You don't."

They stayed that way for a few moments in silence. Trevor kept his gaze averted, looking at the way their hands fit together.

"Trev, come on. Sit back down and stay. I wasn't lying to you the other day when I said I feel a connection to you." He squeezed Trevor's hand, then pulled him to the bedside, placing Trevor's hand against his heart. "That reputation was well earned but came from a place of hurt. It fit the way I lived then, but it doesn't seem to fit so well since I met you."

Trevor looked down into Clive's handsome face and earnest expression. This wasn't a line or a bucket of bullshit. This was true and as honest as Clive could be. It was there in his eyes.

"And when I leave? What then? You go back into your old patterns, and I fall into mine?"

Clive closed his eyes. "I don't want to think about it now. It hurts too badly."

Trevor clamped his back teeth together to keep from telling Clive he might be falling in love with him. For now, he'd keep all opinions, plans, and possible outcomes to himself. There was no sense in making himself crazy or Clive nervous if they didn't make it for the long term, or even the short term.

"Stay," Clive urged.

Trevor sat, wondering if he'd been asked to stay for now or forever.

Chapter Eighteen

CLIVE WAS released from the hospital a week and a half later.

His first stop hadn't been to the marina or even the resort, but to the jail to see his assailant, Afonso Barros.

He was ushered into a small interview room where Afonso waited for him, chained to the table and shackled to the chair. It might be a bit of overkill, but at least the local authorities were taking Clive's safety to heart.

Air inside the little room was stale, oppressive. Bad vibes shimmered inside that room, and Clive didn't even believe in such nonsense. It smelled like piss and body odor, a bad combination when he was just getting over being ill.

Trevor waited outside in the small waiting area near the station's desk. This was something Clive wanted and needed to do alone. No telling how badly it was going to be or how it might make Clive look. He'd already said way too much to Trevor, and he'd experienced the distance. He couldn't say he liked that one bit.

Clive pulled out the chair across from Afonso and sat. "You want to tell me exactly why you decided to take a stab at me? I, for one, would like to know what I did to piss you off."

Afonso gave him a sneer. There was a world of angry hurt in his eyes. "You don't even remember."

"I know we met before the match at some other time and place. Was it last year?" Clive spread his hands. "I'm not good with names unless I spend a lot of time with someone. I'm sorry. But that doesn't give you the right to try and kill me."

Afonso balled his hands into fists. "I didn't want to kill you. I just wanted you to hurt. Like I hurt. You robbed me of glory, then you loved me and threw me away like I was nothing. Then you come back only to flaunt your new lover in my face and humiliate me a second time."

Clive closed his eyes. *Shit.* He had fucked him. Hard. Fast. And good. "I didn't throw you away. I never heard from you again. How was I to know you wanted more unless you said? I'm not a mind reader, and I don't make a habit of chasing after people who don't want me."

Afonso turned his face away. A lone tear ran down his cheek. He sucked his lips in.

"Talk to me, dammit."

Afonso looked back up. The anger still shone in his dark eyes. "My family, they don't know I like men. They would be ashamed of me if they knew. But that didn't matter. You came into that ring like a bronze god, and I wanted. You loved me, and still I wanted. I tried to forget you, and you are always there in my mind, making me want more." He held up a hand as far as the restraints would allow. "I fought it. I conquered your memory until you agreed to defend your title. Then I saw you, then I saw him, and it all came back." His eyes narrowed. "And you looked happy with him. Not lust. Joy. You did not look like that with me. You only wanted a quick fuck, but you didn't want me. Only a body to come in."

The words stung all the more for the truth in them. Clive had never once considered how he'd played with others' hearts. He always assumed the liaisons were a mutually agreed upon means to sexual satisfaction without strings. It had never occurred to him that maybe some of his lovers didn't feel the same.

"Look, I'm sorry your family doesn't know or wouldn't understand. I can't help you with that—my own only pretended understanding until it became inconvenient to do so. I have no advice to give you. However, I can apologize if my behavior last year caused you pain or hurt. It wasn't my intention. If you had come to me back then and explained your feelings, we could have talked it out. Now you've let things fester until you've done something you'll have to pay for. Do you think your family is going to be proud of you now?" Clive held up a hand when it looked like Afonso would answer. "If Trevor hadn't been standing next to me on the dock, I would have died by your hand. You'd be facing a lot heavier charges than you are now."

Afonso shook his head. "I didn't want you to die. I just wanted to cut away the memory of you. To make sure you are human."

Okay… now the guy was talking crazy, but it was probably better to just gloss over that and cut to the chase. He'd apologized for hurting Afonso. What else could he do?

"I'm very human, and I have faults as big as anyone. Maybe more so in this case." Clive touched the bandage on his side. "I've paid for mine; it's time you paid for yours."

Afonso hung his head. His shoulders shook as he began to sob. It was time for Clive to take his leave.

THE HOMECOMING was unbelievable. Trevor suggested they take a boat around the island and land at the ferry station so the others didn't know they'd stopped at the jail. That was fine with Clive. It had been an emotional morning, and time on the water would give him a chance to think and clear his head before they returned to the resort.

They were met at the resort ferry station by Marlie, Juan Pablo, Carlos, Phil, and a very excited Rodger, who kept trilling out *"Congratulations! Fucking bastard!"* No party was complete without a foulmouthed parrot, at least not on Santa Juanita.

God, had Clive missed the feathery little guy.

He was ushered into the pool area, where a welcome home fiesta was underway. The noise, the drinks, and the party atmosphere were a wonderful sight after being cooped up in the hospital for so long. It even shook the specter of the depressing scene in the jail from his mind. The fact he'd get to sleep in his own bed that night and be in familiar surroundings was worth everything.

It wasn't until a few hours later, when they were packed up with food from the resort and after a ride on the shuttle up to Clive's door, that he was finally able to relax in the peace and solitude of his own home.

Trevor put the food away while Clive sat in the living room looking at the view off the bluff. It was a tranquil setting that never lost its power to calm him. However, Trevor had been quiet ever since the day he'd come back to the island after Clive had woken up. Trevor hadn't really mentioned the reason for his silence, though Clive knew. He'd stuck his foot in his mouth again.

Damn if it didn't make Clive think the guy shouldn't be spending the last few days of his vacation tending to a man trying to recuperate from a knife wound.

As a matter of fact, Trevor only had a few days left before he had to be home. Everything went tight inside Clive. Fucking Christ, he didn't want to lose him. Not ever. But he was too afraid to say anything. Afraid Trevor would walk away and never come back.

Clive swallowed down his fear and broached the subject. "Are you excited to see the States again?"

Trevor stalled while putting something away in the fridge. Clive might not be able to see him from where he sat, but he had a great view into the kitchen from the reflection on the sliders.

"I don't know if I'd call it excited. It's going to be weird mostly and a bit sad."

Clive didn't dare to hope Trevor might miss him, but that's what he implied. Right? Ah, hell, he'd take the plunge. "If it's any consolation, I'm going to miss you too."

This time Trevor came out of the kitchen to stand in the doorway. He leaned against the wall, looking sexy as hell. "I quit my job."

Clive's heart skipped a beat. He sat up as straight as his injury allowed. "You did what?"

"Well, not yet. I didn't want to do it over e-mail, fax, or phone. I did, however, type up my resignation. I'll turn it in when I get back." Trevor pushed off from the wall and came to the couch. He took a seat next to Clive.

"What are you going to do after that?" Clive's belly rumbled and his hands began to sweat.

Trevor turned to Clive with a thousand-watt grin. "I understand there's this little island off the coast of Brazil that's looking for a doctor for their clinic."

It was Clive's turn to freeze, but not for long. Despite the pain in his side, he pulled Trevor to him for a kiss.

When he broke away, he spoke against Trevor's lips. "Are you serious? You want to move here? Live here?"

"I am."

"Why didn't you say anything?" Clive moved his hand behind Trevor's head, holding him there so he could see his face and read the truth in his eyes up close.

"I didn't know how." Trevor backed up a little. "Please don't think I'm inviting myself to stay here. If I get the job, it comes with quarters for the doc. I could stay there until I found another place. Of course, I still have to go about getting my license down here, and there is the small matter of me not actively practicing for a while, though I have kept my credentials up-to-date."

"So you said." Clive took a deep breath. The injury pinched and pulled, but he didn't seem to mind it much now—not when he knew Trevor was going to give up his life back in the States for him. To be with *him*. And he didn't ask or beg or plead. The sacrifice had been made willingly and because he wanted to.

Clive just had to be sure he wasn't dreaming—that he hadn't heard wrong. "You really want to stay here? Live here?"

Trevor laughed. "Yes." He cupped Clive's shoulder in his hand and squeezed. "I realized after I came back from the hospital that day that I didn't want to lose you. I might not have known you long, but I know you enough to realize my life is better with you than without you."

Humbled, Clive took as deep a breath as he could manage. "I know what you mean. I didn't want you to go. Hell, I'm not going to like you leaving just to straighten out your affairs back home."

"It won't be for long. Maybe a month or so." Trevor's smile devastated. His dimple ran deep, and his eyes kind of sparkled with happiness.

Everything inside Clive melted to a runny goo. Oh, yeah, a month without seeing that face and touching that body—it was going to be long all right. But the reward at the end would be so worth it. "Maybe I'll fly up and help you pack. Make sure you move faster."

Trevor laughed. "I'd like that. My parents would love to meet you."

Surprisingly enough Clive wanted to meet them too. As corny as it sounded, he needed to thank them for raising such a remarkable and wonderful son. For giving him a chance to fall in love with the one person to turn him from a man of noncommitment to one who wanted nothing more than to wake up to one special man for the rest of his life.

Trevor might have come down to the island to save his own skin, but he'd turned around and saved Clive's in more ways than one. It was a service Clive intended to repay for the rest of their lives.

CASSIE SWEET lives and works from her home office in the New Jersey Highlands, where she shares space with her overaffectionate Golden Retriever and artist husband. Her writing takes her to many destinations, both real and imagined. You can catch her on Twitter under her other writing personae @MKMancosKScott and on Facebook under Kathleen Scott/MK Mancos Author Page.

http://www.mystickat.com/

https://www.facebook.com/MKMancosKScott

Book One: Alchemists and Elementals series

Cassie Sweet

Eye of Truth

ALCHEMISTS AND ELEMENTALS BOOK ONE

http://www.dreamspinnerpress.com

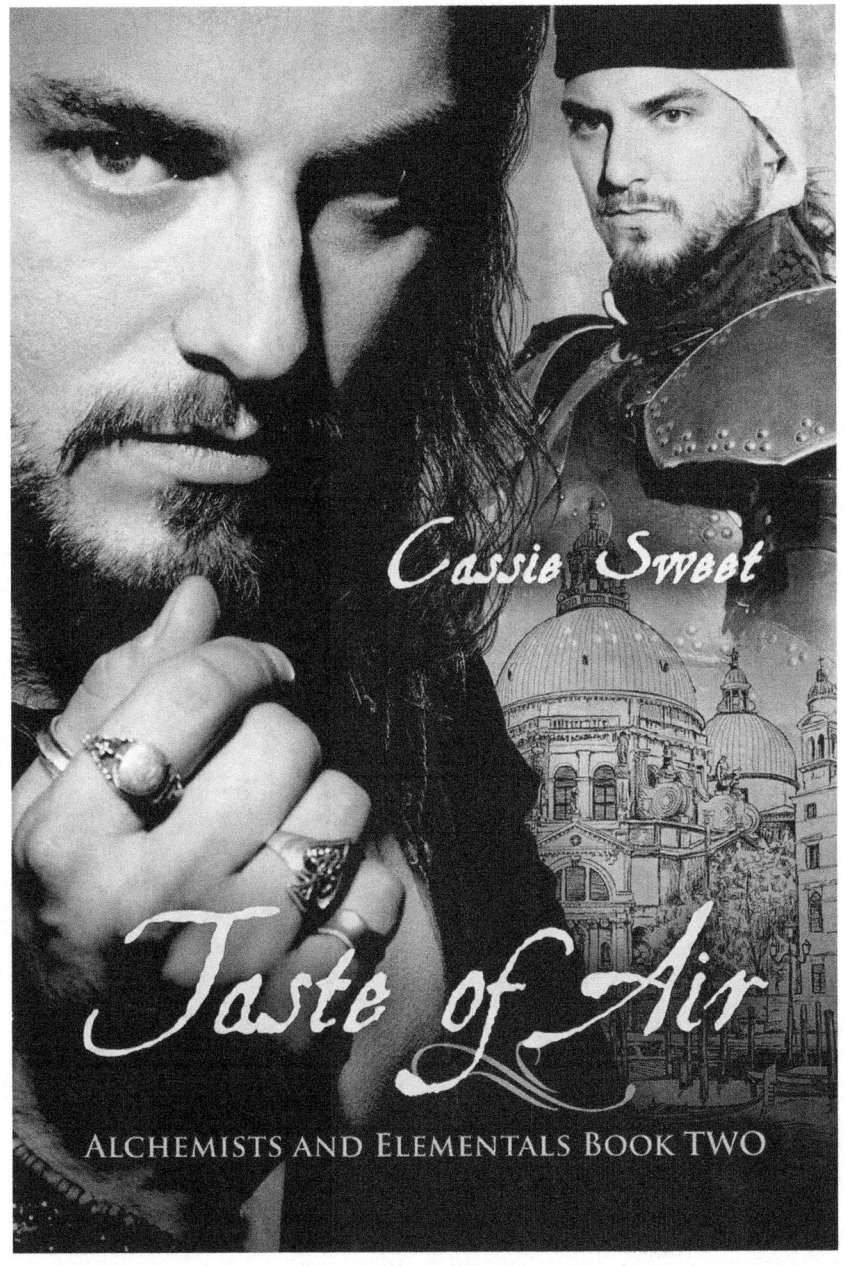

Cassie Sweet

Taste of Air

ALCHEMISTS AND ELEMENTALS BOOK TWO

http://www.dreamspinnerpress.com

OUTING THE QUARTERBACK

TARA LAIN

LONG PASS CHRONICLES

http://www.dreamspinnerpress.com

KIM FIELDING

http://www.dreamspinnerpress.com

Made in United States
Orlando, FL
22 March 2026

79557848R00115